THE BETROTHAL OF A BARON

LINDA RAE SANDE

The Betrothal of a Baron

V1

Cover photograph © PeriodImages

Cover design by Wicked Smart Designs.

https://lindaraesande.com

ISBN: 978-1-946271-81-5

ALSO BY LINDA RAE SANDE

The Daughters of the Aristocracy

The Kiss of a Viscount

The Grace of a Duke

The Seduction of an Earl

The Sons of the Aristocracy

Tuesday Nights

The Widowed Countess

My Fair Groom

The Sisters of the Aristocracy

The Story of a Baron

The Passion of a Marquess

The Desire of a Lady

The Brothers of the Aristocracy

The Love of a Rake

The Caress of a Commander

The Epiphany of an Explorer

The Widows of the Aristocracy

The Gossip of an Earl

The Enigma of a Widow

The Secrets of a Viscount

The Widowers of the Aristocracy

The Dream of a Duchess

The Vision of a Viscountess

The Conundrum of a Clerk
The Charity of a Viscount

The Cousins of the Aristocracy
The Promise of a Gentleman
The Pride of a Gentleman

The Holidays of the Aristocracy
The Christmas of a Countess
The Knot of a Knight
The Holiday of a Marquess
The Snow Angel of a Duke

The Heirs of the Aristocracy
The Angel of an Astronomer
The Puzzle of a Bastard
The Choice of a Cavalier
The Bargain of a Baroness
The Jewel of an Earl's Heir
The Vixen of a Viscount
The Honor of an Heir
The Rose of a Sultan's Son

The Ladies of the Aristocracy
The Lady of a Grump
The Lady of a Sultan
The Wager of a Wallflower

Beyond the Aristocracy
The Pleasure of a Pirate
The Making of a Mistress
The Bride of a Baronet

The Caton of a Captain

Puss and Pots

The Betrothal of a Baron

Stella of Akrotiri

Origins

Deminon

Diana

The Lyon's Den (Dragonblade Publishing)

The Courage of a Lyon

The Lady of a Lyon

Note: Translations of select titles are available in German, Italian, Spanish and Portuguese.

CHAPTER 1
AN INVITATION ON A
RAINY DAY

June 1816, the rainiest month in England's history

For the briefest of moments, Baron David Engleston was sure the sun had made an appearance through the gray clouds that hovered over his manor house near Kent. A rare event given it hadn't stopped raining for more than a few hours for the entire month of June.

He rushed to the window in his study and stared out in an attempt to catch a glimpse, but it was too late. A shroud once again hid the ball of light.

"Should we build an ark, sir?" Peters asked from the study's threshold.

David gave his portly butler a quelling glance as he tightened his greatcoat around his body. Despite the constant fires that had been set in all the fireplaces of Engleston Park, a chill still permeated the air. "How are the horses?" he asked, worried the stable might have flooded by now.

"Mr. Cooper let them out. Said they were restless," Peters replied, referring to the groom who saw to the six geldings, two shires, and a single stallion that made up the bulk of the animals on the estate. A few chickens, a single cow, and the sheepdog, who at that moment could be found under David's desk, made up the rest. The dog had been keeping his feet warm that morning as he saw to updating the estate's ledgers.

"I know how they feel," David replied. "Has Mr. Tuttlebaum paid a call?" The farmer was one of three who worked the farmlands to the east of Engleston Park. Their tenant cottages were located on the outskirts of the nearest village. David feared the thatched roofs of the two-room domiciles might have begun to leak. If he had to pay for repairs, the emergency funds he had set aside upon the death of his father would be nearly depleted.

"He's in the kitchens with Mrs. Wright," Peters replied.

David's eyes narrowed. "Why didn't you inform me he was here?"

The butler's eyes darted to the right before he said, "He asked that he be allowed a few minutes alone with the housekeeper before I announced him."

Blinking, David considered this bit of news before his eyes rounded. "Is he *finally* proposing marriage?" he asked in alarm. His oldest tenant farmer had held a candle for his housekeeper for as long as he had been a baron, a title he had inherited when his father died of pneumonia ten years earlier.

The reminder of marriage had David wincing. At thirty-three years of age, he had yet to take a wife, which meant he didn't have an heir. The nursery on the third floor of the country manor remained as it had been when he was but a young boy, as did the nursery in the family's townhouse in Westminster.

"One can only hope, my lord," Peters replied on a long sigh. "Given the poor growing season, he may be asking that she wait yet another year."

David grimaced. Although he didn't rely entirely on the income from the crops grown at Engleston Park to make his living, his tenant farmers did. Everything that had been planted in March and April had drowned with the incessant rains. In an effort to stave off complete starvation, he had funded the building of several greenhouses near the tenant cottages and ordered that the farmers grow whatever they could beneath the oil cloth-covered buildings.

That had been a month ago.

"Do you suppose he's done with his proposal?" David asked, nodding in the direction of the kitchens. He almost envied the farmer. Not only had Tuttlebaum found a potential wife, he was in the warmest room of the house. "Because I could really use a cup of tea about now, and I'd like to drink it in the kitchens."

"Of course, my lord," Peters replied. He stepped aside as David made his way out of the study and down the long corridor leading to the back of the house.

In the past, he would have paused before the portrait of his late father to regard the familiar visage—one he stared at every morning in a mirror whilst he was shaving.

Today he stopped to regard the painting next to it, one of his mother. Lady Eva Engleston was still alive, preferring to live in London year-round. Although David had feared she would spend her inheritance quickly and require him to support her, she had surprised him by practicing frugality in her purchases. "I'm no longer invited to all the best balls," she told him on one occasion. "And unlike most of my ilk, I am not beholden to the latest fashions from Paris."

At the time, David remembered telling her she could buy whatever she liked. He could afford it.

Now... now he wasn't so sure. This year's income from his business in London was at risk. Rain had put a damper on shopping and threatened the livelihood of anyone who depended on farming for their incomes. The lack of good crops from the year before certainly didn't help the situation. Food was expensive, and the chilly weather meant everyone was forced to buy more coal for their fireplaces. Only those who owned coal mines would see a profit this year.

As he stared at Lady Engleston, David wondered if he would be lucky enough to find a woman as steadfast and as wise as his mother. If he did, would she be able to live with him?

Would he be able to live with her?

At the moment, he realized he would have to do so. He couldn't afford to hire a mistress, let alone pay the rent on a townhouse and cover the cost of her modiste and fripperies.

How did other aristocrats manage when their incomes were at risk?

He found Mr. Tuttlebaum seated at the trestle in the middle of the room where the servants ate their meals. Hat in hand, the man appeared as if he had lost his best friend.

"Did she say 'no'?" David asked as he stopped before the dejected man.

Frank Tuttlebaum glanced up, obviously startled to discover the owner of his farmlands regarding him with an expression of worry. He quickly stood and gave a short bow. "I didn't ask Mrs. Wright for her hand, my lord," he replied.

David leaned over to glance through the arched doorway that led to the kitchens. When he didn't spy the housekeeper, he turned his attention back to the farmer. "Why ever not? I thought you two would be wed by now."

Frank's eyes rounded as his face took on the color of a beet. "Oh, well, I told her I intend to, sir," he said. "So as she doesn't go acceptin' someone else's suit 'afore mine."

Angling his head to one side, David prompted, "And?"

"She sounded disappointed but not surprised, sir."

"So... what has you looking so glum?"

Sighing loudly, the farmer pulled out a few missives from

his coat pocket and held them out to David. "Oh, it's just the infernal weather, sir. Although it has given me the chance to sharpen the blades and do some indoor repairs." He forced a grin. "The mail coach stopped in the village, and seein' how I was there, I told the driver I could deliver these here letters to you."

"Thank you," David replied, rifling through the envelopes. Nothing looked important, but he recognized the writing on one as belonging to a good friend in London. "How are the greenhouses working out?"

"Oh, very good, sir. The stuff we planted is startin' to come up just fine, and those lemon trees you gave us from your orangery are looking right as rain." He winced. "Pardon the pun, sir."

David chuckled. "Well, see to it you get some luncheon before you head back out there," he said, glad when the cook appeared with a steaming cup of tea and set it on the trestle.

"Afternoon, my lord," she said as she dipped a curtsy. "Would you like tea?"

"It's why I've come," David acknowledged.

"I can bring it to your study, sir," she offered.

"I would prefer to drink it where it will stay warm," he replied, setting the missives on the table so he could remove his coat. "If Mr. Tuttlebaum doesn't mind a bit of company."

Franks' eyes rounded again. "Oh, I don't mind at all, sir," he said.

"I'll see to it right away," Margaret said before she turned to Frank and added, "I've got some cheese and a dish of beef soup about ready for you."

"Much appreciated, Margaret," Frank replied.

"Soup sounds good for me, too, if there's enough," David said, his stomach growling despite the breakfast she had made for him earlier that morning.

"Of course there is, sir, although you'll be having it again with your dinner tonight," she warned. She disappeared into the kitchens as David broke the wax seals from his letters.

As he unfolded the one from his friend, a pasteboard creme calling card fell onto the table. He picked it up and studied the engraved script. The words "Soho Club" and its address were printed on one side along with the words "Show for admittance" in much smaller print at the bottom.

Curious as to why his friend would send the card, he took a moment to read the letter.

> *Dear Lord Engleston,*
>
> *I hope this letter finds you high and dry. I understand you have suffered as much rain as we have here in the capital. Glum weather begets gloomy friends, hence I have decided it is time we hole up at the Soho Club for a few days of games and dancing.*
>
> *You're not that far away, there is nothing of importance happening with this much rain falling, and you are not wed, so you have no excuse not to join us. The games begin Tuesday afternoon. Bring your pennies, and we may even play for money. Oh, and bring the card. You'll need it for admittance to the club and your room.*
>
> *Sincerely yours,*
>
> *Dicky*
>
> *Post scriptum. If you're still unwed, perhaps we can find you a suitable bride here in London before you return to Engleston Park. About damned time you be betrothed. You're not getting any younger.*

Chuckling at the insistent tone of the letter as well as by Richard Copper's postscript, David was at first tempted to send his regrets. Although he really should be on the hunt for a bride, he had thought to put it off until the next Season started. The reminder of rain in the capital had him reconsidering. If other aristocrats were suffering crop losses due to all the rain, they might not have the funds to offer decent dowries. Given his dwindling bank account, David was afraid he would require part of a dowry to get by until the weather improved.

He once again glanced at the Soho Club card as he considered his decision. Richard, Earl of Penhurst, had a point. The weather had made him glum. Perhaps a trip to London would do him some good. Give him an opportunity to pay a call on his tailor and visit his favorite stationer. Mayhap take in a show at one of the theatres with his mother. Enjoy some cards and dancing at the Soho Club. If he wasn't happy with the accommodations, he could always stay in his rooms at the Cleveland Row townhouse where he lived during the Season.

When Margaret delivered a tea tray complete with biscuits and cake along with bowls of soup for both he and Frank, David felt decidedly warmer.

The two men enjoyed their luncheons in relative quiet, each lost in their own thoughts about their immediate futures as unmarried men.

David was quite sure Frank Tuttlebaum had some experience when it came to women. When he was younger, the farmer had been a strapping lad, attracting the attention of the girls in the nearby village. He continued to enjoy female companionship throughout his middle years. Now that he was older, he was finally of a mind to take a wife.

As for David, painful shyness and a gangly body had prevented him from enjoying those same attentions. By the time he had inherited the barony, though, his frame and face had filled out so he looked more like his father had at that age. Taking his place in Parliament had forced him to speak with the other lords. Forced him to learn the basics of conversing with his peers.

However, if a woman so much as looked at him, other than in a dance where the moves prevented easy banter, he glanced away or hurried off. The alternative—to stand his ground and actually carry on his side of a conversation—wasn't something he could abide. As a result, David found himself at the age of thirty-three not only unmarried, but inexperienced when it came to bedding a woman.

The Rt. Honorable Lord Engleston, sixth baron Engleston, was still a virgin.

CHAPTER 2
A CLUB REVEALS SOME SECRETS

The following Tuesday, Soho Square, London

As the Engleston traveling coach ambled over the cobblestone streets toward the Soho Club, David gazed out the rain-streaked window. Despite a relatively clear morning, muddy roads had slowed the horses once they were out of Kent. When they reached the outskirts of London, a fine drizzle began to fall. At least the four-hour trip afforded him time to review business ledgers and read a book.

"I'll see to it your trunk is left with a footman, milord," his driver, Carver, said as he opened the coach door. "Then I'll pull into the mews around back."

Before David had stepped out of the equipage, though, two footmen approached and saw to removing the trunk from the back of the coach. Carver's mouth dropped open in awe.

Remembering he needed to show the creme calling card, David fished it from his waistcoat pocket and held it out to one of the footmen.

"We're expecting you, my lord," the taller footman said. "Welcome to the Soho Club."

For a moment, David wondered how the servant knew

who he was. Then, when his driver shut the coach door, he knew why. The Engleston barony crest was emblazoned in gold paint on the coach door. Although it was a bit mud-splattered, it was still readable. "Thank you. Where...?" He regarded the property tucked into the corner of the square with a furrowed brow. At first glance, he didn't see an obvious entrance to the club—there was no shingle or a placard to indicate the name of the establishment—but a liveried man was posted next a set of doors marked "Private."

"Right there, milord," the shorter footman said as he pointed to the entrance. "Mr. Peabody will see to your coat and provide directions to reach Mrs. Skarsgard. She'll have the key to your room."

David nodded his understanding and made his way to the entrance. He held out his card, and the portly servant opened the door. "I'm looking for Mrs. Skarsgard," he said, once he was inside the wood-paneled vestibule. He couldn't help but notice the number of greatcoats hung on a series of hooks, and the bin for umbrellas was nearly full. The desk off to the side was unmanned.

"Would you like to leave your coat, my lord?"

Allowing Mr. Peabody to assist with his greatcoat, David shrugged out of it and dropped his umbrella into the bin.

The servant opened the next door, revealing what appeared to be an inner sanctum. Candle-lit sconces cast a warm glow along the walls while velvet drapes covered every window. Several chandeliers added their golden light and warmth, which had David thinking he had stepped into the club's ballroom. An empty one, though, for no one else was there despite an array of upholstered furnishings.

"You can find Mrs. Skarsgard up the stairs and down the hall," Mr. Peabody said before he bowed and disappeared through the door from which they had just come.

David turned and made his way up the stairs, his footfalls silent on the thick Aubusson carpeting.

At the top of the stairs, there was only one direction in which to go, and he made his way down the carpeted corridor until he came upon a door bearing a brass nameplate. He knocked, relieved when a feminine voice said, "Come."

Opening it only a fraction, David dared a glance inside before he fully stepped into a well-appointed office. There were two wingback chairs and a small table. A chaise longue sat beneath one of the room's two windows. Given the gray beyond the glass, the room was mostly lit with candle lamps.

The source of the feminine voice sat at a small escritoire. She stood upon his arrival, though. "Welcome to the Soho Club," she said by way of a greeting.

"I'm to ask for Mrs. Skarsgard," David said, holding out the creme card. Despite his discomfort whilst in the company of the opposite sex, he did his best to keep his gaze on the woman.

"And found her you have," she replied. Set off by a pale yellow day gown, black hair, and chocolate brown eyes, Mrs. Skarsgard's caramel skin fairly glowed in the candlelight. It was impossible to tell her age. She could have been twenty, thirty, or forty years old.

"It's good to make your acquaintance. I am Lord—"

"We don't use names here, sir," Mrs. Skarsgard interrupted. "Which allows our members to be whomever they wish to be without any societal expectations."

David gave a start. "Then how am I to claim the room that has apparently been reserved for me by Lord... Dicky?" he asked, deciding if he couldn't use Richard's real name, he would try using his nickname.

"We've been expecting you," Mrs. Skarsgard stated. She lifted a key from the escritoire and held it out to him. "Near the end of the hall on the right. I'm afraid the room doesn't off much of a vantage," she added as David took the proffered key. "But it is private. Breakfast is served whenever you would like it in the dining room, or if you wish, a tray can be delivered to your room." She paused as she glanced at a parchment from her desk. "As I understand the arrangement, you'll be with us for three nights."

David nodded. "Thank you, yes," he replied. "Are there any rules I should know about?"

"No names. No sharing what you might see or hear whilst you're under our roof, and you can be assured of the same consideration from our other club members."

Members.

David was about to mention he wasn't a member when Mrs. Skarsgard said, "You are a member of the Soho Club during your stay, of course, and you are welcome to return when you're able. You need only show your card." She held it out for him.

Giving a slight bow as he retrieved the card, David said, "I appreciate the consideration."

"Oh," Mrs. Skarsgard said as she suddenly held up a finger. "You needn't feel the least bit shy when you're in the company of our members, especially the women. Remember, nothing you say or hear will be revealed beyond the walls of the club."

Blinking at hearing the comment, David wondered if Dicky had made mention of his problem with shyness or if the woman had sorted it of her own accord. "Good to know," he replied, well aware of how his face was reddening. "Might you know where Lord... uh, where my host can be found?"

Mrs. Skarsgard angled her head to one side, as if she were listening intently to something beyond the door. "You'll find him downstairs in the card room engaged in a game of whist."

Chuckling, David once again nodded and said his thanks before he backed out of the office. For a moment, he thought to head downstairs to find the Earl of Penhurst, but instead he decided to leave his valise in his room. Unsure of what he would find beyond the wood door—rooms in coaching inns were always a bit dodgy—he turned the key and was pleasantly surprised to discover his room was as elegant as any master bedchamber in a Mayfair mansion.

Besides the Turkish carpeting decorating the floor, the bed was dressed in a blue velvet counterpane and the masculine furnishings were of a dark wood. The room's only window was covered in blue velvet drapes, and a quick glance out proved Mrs. Skarsgard's assessment regarding its lack of a vantage—the brick wall of another building stood a few feet beyond the glass, but there were no matching windows to cause concerns when it came to privacy.

As he was setting his valise on the bed, David noticed his trunk had already been delivered and was dry. Impressed by the service, he went about unpacking some clothes for that evening's entertainments. His butler, who also acted as his valet when he was at his estate in Kent, had included the usual assortment of breeches, shirts, cravats, and waistcoats suitable for wear during the day. In addition, there was his more formal attire—satin breeches and topcoat, stockings, dance shoes, and the most flamboyant waistcoat he owned.

Girding his loins for what was to come—he expected he would be introduced to people he didn't know—David took one look in the bathing chamber mirror to ensure he was presentable and then opened the door.

At the very same moment, the door to the room adjacent to his opened. A brunette-haired woman, fair of complexion and dressed in a jonquil gown, stepped out and stared at him with wide eyes the color of brandy.

For a moment, David was sure the sun had broken through the clouds. Framed by the pink decor of her room, she appeared as if she was lit from within, and when her glorious smile appeared, it only magnified the effect.

He had no idea of her age—twenty, perhaps?—but he knew at that moment he would have to say something. A greeting at the very least. He swallowed. "Hello," he managed as he nodded.

The brilliant smile brightened. "Oh, by chance, are you my betrothed?" she asked, sounding breathless.

David blinked. And blinked again. "Why, yes. Yes I am," he replied.

CHAPTER 3
A YOUNG LADY MEETS HER MAN

For a moment, Miss Marian Copper wondered how she could have been so bold. So forward. So fast. So outlandish.

Nervousness, of course. That could be the only explanation for why she would blurt out such a query to a man she had never seen before, let alone met.

Perhaps there was hope in her anxiousness, though, too. The gentleman who stared at her in surprise was rather handsome and not nearly as old as she'd been led to believe. His dark hair wasn't cut into the latest style, but a Titus would not have suited him nor the dark eyebrows and shorter sideburns framing a kind face. While his navy topcoat and Nankeen breeches were typical for a man of his age, his rust colored silk waistcoat featured embroidered flowers.

From his hesitant but pleased expression—Marian realized she had surprised him with her sudden appearance—she knew he hadn't paid witness to her watching him when he entered the club and made his way up the main stairs to Mrs. Skarsgard's office.

She could have simply waited to be introduced to the

gentleman when he came downstairs to join the card game already in progress. Curiosity had her excusing herself from her uncle's table, though, and making her way back to her room whilst the newcomer acquired the key to his.

She rather hoped his room was better suited to him than hers was to her. When she had opened the door to it for the first time the day before, she wasn't prepared for the overwhelming first impression that she had either entered a very young girl's bedchamber or a brothel.

Not that she knew what a brothel looked like. Obviously she had never stepped foot into such a scandalous establishment. But the thought had been there nonetheless.

What else could explain the soft pink silk on the walls? The deep pink velvet counterpane and drapes? The deeper pink curtains around the bed? The gold gilt dressing table and three-paneled japanned screen in the corner? The only redeeming feature of so much pink was that when she regarded her reflection in the cheval mirror set into one corner of the room, her complexion appeared far more "peaches and cream" than usual.

Perhaps her yellow gown was helping in that regard, too.

Uncle had told her to pack her very brightest and colorful gowns. To wear something cheerful on this day. Something to counter the gloomy weather beyond the glass windows.

She had been about to remind him young ladies weren't really allowed to wear bright colors when he surprised her with a pasteboard box from Madame Suzanne's in Oxford Street. Inside, wrapped in white tissue paper, was the very gown she was now wearing, a jonquil muslin confection adorned with embroidered flowers.

Flowers that looked as if they could have been created by the very same seamstress that had made Lord Engleston's waistcoat.

"Although..."

The word brought Marian out of her reverie. The gentleman was still regarding her with an expression of surprise, and the hesitant word had Marian's eyes rounding slightly. "Apologies, sir—"

"Please, do not," he interrupted before he winced. "Your words were entirely unexpected but rather welcome just then."

Marian swallowed. "They were?" She watched as the baron's face visibly reddened.

"As were you... a... a ray of sunshine on a rather gray day," he stammered. "Oh, dear. I am making a cake of this, aren't I?"

Blinking, Marian shook her head. "Oh, not at all, sir. My uncle will be pleased to learn his gift—this gown—is accomplishing its intention."

"Gown?" the baron repeated. His gaze traveled down and then back up before his face once again brightened. "Oh, indeed," he said, nodding. "Yellow is a good choice on such a rainy day." He once again winced, as if he regretted his attempt at conversation.

Marian beamed in delight, heartened to realize that *she* had been the ray of sunshine and not her gown. "My uncle will be pleased to hear it," she said. "He had it made for me. For this occasion."

The baron blinked. "Oh? The occasion of meeting me?" he asked, obviously confused. His eyes darted sideways, as if he was attempting to sort who her uncle might be. "Or... are we already acquainted?" he added before his face once again reddened. "Oh, I suppose if we're betrothed, we must be," he reasoned. "I apologize if we've been introduced—"

"We have not been, my lord," Marian quickly said, her own face heating at hearing the reminder of her earlier words. She was beginning to understand that the gentleman's nervousness was most probably due to shyness.

Her uncle had warned her the baron did not easily converse with those he didn't know.

"Oh," he replied. He glanced around. "There doesn't appear to be anyone to do the honors of a proper introduction."

"Oh, my uncle will see to it. When we're downstairs," she said. "Although..."

"Mrs. Skarsgard said we weren't to use names," he remembered.

"Exactly," she said with a good deal of disappointment.

His brows furrowed. "But... say we *were* betrothed—"

"Aren't we?"

He blinked. "Yes. Yes, we are," he agreed, apparently deciding to play along. "I have heard some men refer to their... to their wives as 'sweetings'," he murmured.

"My sweet," she stated. When she saw his look of bewilderment, she added, "I would prefer 'my sweet' over 'sweeting' as I think 'sweeting' makes it sound as if I'm some sort of bird. Or a cat."

His mouth rounded before he nodded. "You have a very good point. And I do think 'my sweet' makes it sound as if you're a special treat. Like a candy at Christmas," he reasoned.

Marian displayed a brilliant grin. "Exactly," she replied. "Now... what shall I call you?"

She watched as the baron seemed to struggle. "I could call you 'dear'," she offered when he didn't offer an endearment.

"You could," he agreed, but he showed not the least bit of enthusiasm for the term. "My first thought when I hear it is the animal, though," he added. "The doe. Not the buck." He once again winced, but Marian understood his reasoning perfectly.

"What about 'my dearest'?" she asked.

"Oh, I like that," he said. "Especially if it's true."

"Well, of course it is," she replied. "You're my betrothed," she added, rather enjoying their secret conversation.

It was the baron's turn to display a brilliant grin. "I shall answer to that then," he stated. He reached for her hand and lifted it to his lips. "It's very good to meet you, my sweet," he said before he bent and brushed his lips over the back of her knuckles.

A pleasant tremor shot up Marian's arm as she watched the baron bow over her hand. "And you, my dearest," she said as she dipped a curtsy. She didn't care that he continued to hold onto her hand even after he straightened. That his gaze had gone to her lips, which had parted slightly. Without her realizing it, the tip of her tongue touched her top lip. She didn't mean it as an invitation for him to kiss her, but she was heartened when it seemed to do the trick.

The baron hesitated, as if he was having an internal war with himself. Determined they kiss, Marian reached up with her free hand to place it against the side of his face while she stood on tiptoes. "Kiss me," she whispered, not making it a question.

"If you're sure," he murmured.

The pressure on her lips was so tentative, so light, Marian wondered at first if they were even touching. And then she knew they were, for she felt the firm pads of his against the soft pillows of hers, and all at once they seemed to gently lock into place.

She instinctively knew what to do, and apparently the baron knew as well, for she felt the slight suckling and a pleasant sensation that had her insides fizzing with excitement. There was a moment when time seemed to stop, and all that existed were only the two of them.

One of his hands had moved to cup her jaw, and she was glad of the support. In need of more, she leaned forward and gripped one of the lapels of the shawl collar of his topcoat.

When their bodies met—her chest into his middle—a warmth permeated her entire being.

She mewled her disappointment when he pulled his lips from hers, but even if he hadn't, she would have had to, for she needed to take a deep breath.

The two stared at one another for several seconds before she said, "Thank you."

His eyes rounded. "It is I who should thank you," he whispered. "I've never..." He clamped his mouth shut. "That is to say, I am terribly out of practice."

"I wouldn't have guessed it, but then, I've never been kissed before," she replied with a shrug.

Blinking, he said, "You haven't?"

Shaking her head, she gave him a prim grin. "Do you suppose we might do it again... sometime... soon?"

Although his hand had moved from her jaw to her shoulder, the two hadn't stepped apart from one another. They would have continued to stand impossibly close for who knows how long except that the voices of two gentlemen carrying on a conversation were growing closer. At any moment, the men would be at the top of the stairs, able to pay witness to Marian and the baron in the state of a near embrace.

Marian didn't wish to give up her hold on the man. His door was shut, but hers was still open. Tugging on his shawl collar, she stepped back and into her room, which forced the baron to swing around. Just before the intruders arrived at the top of the stairs, Marian kicked her door shut with a slippered foot. Before the baron could put voice to a protest or question what was happening, she had a hand behind his neck and was pulling his head down for another kiss.

The baron obliged, his lips obviously hungry for hers. They stood kissing for nearly an entire minute before they broke the kiss at the same time.

Staring at her for a moment, he seemed at a loss for

words. He lifted his head and allowed his gaze to sweep the bedchamber. "Wh… where are we?"

"My room," Marian replied. "It's terribly pink, I know," she added, managing to make it sound as if pink was her least favorite color.

"I've never been in a woman's bedchamber before," he whispered, an expression of worry settling on his features.

A knock at the door had them both giving a start. "Who is it?" she called out, managing to far calmer than she felt.

"Marian, your presence is needed for this next game of cards," came a male voice.

From the baron's expression—his brows had shot up and the look of worry turned to alarm—Marian realized their tryst had to end. "I'll be right down, Uncle," she replied, although she visibly winced.

"Is everything all right?" From the concern in the older male's voice, it was apparent he suspected something was amiss.

The baron quickly changed places with Marian and gave her a nod as he tucked himself into the corner behind the door. He reached over, turned the handle, and opened the door as Marian positioned herself at the opening. "Everything is fine, Uncle. I had a tear in my stocking and wished to change it is all," she added as she pushed the door open even more and stepped out. She glanced down the corridor, and not seeing another gentleman—she was sure her uncle had been speaking with someone as he climbed the stairs—she asked, "Did the viscount come up with you?"

Richard, Earl of Penhurst, motioned to one of the doors down the corridor. "Huntley had to return to his room. We had a bit of excitement, and he spilled some brandy. Wanted to change his breeches."

Marian turned and closed the door before placing her hand on the older gentleman's arm. "I didn't realize a game of whist could cause such a sensation," she teased.

"It wasn't the cards, darling," her uncle said with a chuckle. "It was my declaration that I intend to see Lord Engleston betrothed before he returns to Kent. Huntley laughed so hard I think he hurt himself."

Furrowing her brows, Marian glanced up at him. "Ah. He is the baron you spoke of a few days ago, is he not?"

"Indeed," Richard replied. "I look forward to introducing you two."

As they took the turn to go down the stairs, Marian dared a glance toward the end of the corridor and discovered her door was slightly open. Obviously the baron was still in her room, attempting to eavesdrop on her conversation with her uncle. In a slightly louder than usual voice, she said, "I don't know why Lord Huntley should find it funny. I expect Lord Engleston is an excellent catch."

Richard gave her a curious glance before he said, "I am glad we are in agreement." After a pause, he added, "If you recall, he's one of the gentlemen I thought might suit you."

"Oh, I do recall," Marian replied, her chin lifted high. "Not too old. Not too young." *My dearest.* "What else did you say about him?"

Chuckling, her uncle said, "He's suffers from shyness. My fear is that if you so much as look at him, he'll disappear into the carpet," he warned. "I rather doubt he'll say much, but please don't take it personally."

Marian couldn't help but give her uncle a disbelieving glance. Although the man she had left in her room had been a bit shy with her, he had said far more than three words. And he'd kissed her. Twice.

"What card game are we playing now?" she asked as they made their way toward the card parlor.

"*Vingt-et-un,*" the earl replied. "We require a dealer, and you're rather good at it. This way, we'll be able to include Lord Engleston when he finally makes an appearance."

Marian gave her uncle a grin. "It shouldn't be long. He

has already checked into his room." When the earl gave her a questioning glance, she added, "I might have paid witness to his arrival whilst I was upstairs."

"Oh, did you now?" Richard asked, a smirk appearing. "Well then, the rest of this afternoon will be very interesting."

About to agree, Marian decided it best she keep her secret to herself.

CHAPTER 4
AN EMBOLDENED MAN

*M**eanwhile, back in the pink room*

After the young lady's departure from her room, David Engleston held his breath as he listened to the fading conversation between the woman he now thought of as 'my sweet' and her uncle. In an attempt to hear better, he opened the door and surreptitiously glanced out. The last words he heard were, *I expect Lord Engleston is an excellent catch.*

He leaned his head against the adjacent wall, his heart pounding so hard, he could hear his pulse in his ears.

Bless her heart, he thought.

In desperate need of air, he took a deep breath and let it out, aware of a wonderful floral scent that seemed to suddenly surround him.

Her scent.

He sniffed, determined to catch as much of the sweet air as he could.

Then realization set in, and he grimaced.

His sweet's uncle was Richard Copper, Earl of Penhurst. *Dicky.*

He had wondered why the earl would think it so important David be betrothed by the end of his stay at the

Soho Club. Why he would make mention of it over cards with Lord Huntley.

But why did Huntley find it so amusing?

David dipped his head. "I suppose I deserve that," he murmured to himself. At his age, he really should be married. He should have already started his nursery. Fathered an heir and a spare, shyness be damned.

He dared another glance out the door, and finding the corridor empty, he stepped out of the pink room and closed the wood panel as quietly as he could manage. The floral scent of his sweet once again surrounded him, and he inhaled softly.

Marian.

The earl had called her 'Marian' when he had knocked on the door.

Pausing at his room—he thought it best he take a quick look in a mirror to be sure he was still presentable—David was about to insert his key into the lock when Marcus Smith-Jones, Viscount Huntley, emerged from the next room down the corridor.

"There you are," Marcus said, obviously surprised to see David. "I was beginning to think you hadn't made the trip."

"Oh, how do, Huntley?" David managed, his nervousness returning when he remembered they weren't supposed to be using their real names. "Have you been here long?"

"Oh, all day," Huntley replied. "And you?"

Deciding he didn't need to go back into his room after all, David stepped away from his door and shrugged. "A half-hour, I suppose."

The viscount jerked his head back. "Well, what's kept you?" he asked as the two headed for the stairs. "We had a wicked game of whist going on in the card parlor."

Remembering the reason for Huntley's visit to his room, David decided to forego temerity in favor of vexing the viscount. "Oh? Well, I would have come down sooner, but I wished to spend some time with my betrothed." He angled his head in Huntley's direction as they made their descent and realized it was fortunate they were nearly at the bottom of the stairs.

Marcus, Viscount Huntley, stumbled. His arms flailed as he was forced to turn his body and take several quick steps in the middle of a stair runner before landing on his bum. His feet ended up on the next step down, which meant his knees were bent and spread wide. The distinctive sound of tearing fabric had the man grimacing. Given his pot belly and thin limbs, he looked like a frog with his back leaning against a log.

"Good God, man, are you all right?" David asked in alarm. He reached out a hand to help the viscount.

Marcus stared up at him in disbelief. "Ha! I could swear I heard you say something about your betrothed," he said as he struggled to stand. Even with David's assistance, it was a moment before the viscount was put to rights.

"I did, actually," David replied, feeling rather emboldened.

His brows furrowed, Marcus stared at him a moment. "Well, who is she? What's her name?"

David drew his head back so his single chin became two. "No names. Remember, we're in the Soho Club."

About to put voice to a protest, Marcus couldn't when David headed toward the card parlor. Huffing, Marcus brushed a hand across his behind in an attempt to determine how much damage had been done to his breeches. Deciding his topcoat tails would hide the evidence of the tear, he hurried to catch up to the baron.

David paused on the threshold, a most delicious excitement making him grin when he spotted his betrothed sitting across from Richard, Earl of Penhurst. In a room filled with gentlemen wearing dark topcoats and garish waistcoats of various colors and a few rather conservatively dressed women, Marian shone like a gold foil-backed diamond. She had a deck of cards in one hand and her gaze on a set of three cards she had dealt to the earl.

His shyness nearly returned when she glanced up and gave him a brilliant smile. "Oh, my dearest," she blurted as she dropped the deck of cards to the table and stood.

David gave her a matching grin and hurried to take her hand to his lips. "Oh, my sweet. You look lovelier than when I last saw you," he gushed as he bowed, well aware that Marcus watched from the threshold. As for the others in the room, well, he hadn't noticed there were four other tables of card players engaged in games of whist until the noise in the room died down somewhat at his sudden appearance and declaration.

Across the table, Richard's eyes rounded as David kissed his niece on the cheek. "Engleston? What the—?"

"Remember, no names," David interrupted as he raised a finger in the direction of the earl, his gaze never leaving Marian's. "We're at the Soho Club."

Richard scoffed. "I don't care where we are. You'll unhand Miss Copper this very instant."

Miss Copper. Marian Copper, David reasoned, still holding onto her warm gloved hand. In the brighter lighting of the card parlor, he discovered she was prettier than he remembered. Fairer, too, her features soft and set on a heart-shaped face with translucent skin. Her hair, which had appeared brunette upstairs, was highlighted with strands of gold and mahogany that shimmered under the room's chandelier. "I must say, I'm thrilled you are the uncle of such a fine creature as my sweet," David responded. "Are you also her guardian?"

One of Richard's brows furrowed in suspicion. "I am indeed," he answered slowly.

"Oh, good. Then let us make this betrothal official, shall we?" David went on, emboldened enough to complete the niceties. "Will you give me permission to marry your niece?"

He was aware of his sweet's mouth rounding although her gaze never left him to see that her uncle had settled back in his chair and splayed his fingers on the felt tabletop.

"Well, now that all depends," Richard replied slowly, well aware Viscount Huntley had returned to the chair he had occupied earlier. A quick glance in his direction proved he was experiencing as much disbelief as he was.

"On what?" David asked, finally diverting his gaze from Marian to regard the earl with an arched brow. Richard's attention was on his niece, though, and she tore her gaze from David to stare back at him.

"Indeed, on what?" she asked in dismay.

CHAPTER 5
TERMS AND CONDITIONS APPLY

*D*avid felt a twinge deep in his chest. A sensation he had never before experienced. He had spoken with a woman. He had kissed her. Agreed to make her his wife. And now she was agreeing with him when it came to dealing with her guardian.

Could it be he was already in love with her? Was that even possible? They had only just met!

Richard stared at Marian until she lifted her chin in defiance. "Isn't it far better I marry a man you already know and respect instead of a stranger? One of your friends?" she asked in a quiet voice.

Although most of the other card players in the parlor had returned their attentions to their games, a few were watching and listening to the interchange between Richard, David, and Marian as if the trio were performing a play at one of the nearby theatres.

About to answer, Richard couldn't when one of the female onlookers called out, "I say let her marry him, if she really wants him."

"Me, as well," a man yelled from the next table over.

Murmurs and nods of agreement passed through the other gaming tables as if on a wave.

"I say let him marry her," a male voice said from the far corner.

Holding up a staying hand, Richard directed his answer to the others in the room. "I haven't said they couldn't marry," he claimed. "There might have to be some conditions is all."

"Yeah. A dowry," the first cat-caller said, loud enough for everyone to hear. A chorus of chuckles sounded around the room, although the comment had Richard's brows furrowing deeper than they had been.

"That is a consideration," Richard agreed.

"You set me up," Marcus accused, hitting the earl on the arm with the back of his hand.

"Wot?" Richard turned to stare at the viscount. "I did no such thing."

"Oh, I see how it is," Marcus countered, crossing his arms over his chest so they rested on his protruding belly.

Marian's eyes rounded. "What does he mean by that, Uncle?" she asked.

Before Richard could respond, Marcus said, "We had a wager."

David grasped Marian's gloved hand, glad when she didn't attempt to pull it away. With the attentions of all the onlookers, he wished the floor would swallow him whole. "What sort of wager?" he asked, his manner tentative. He aimed a suspicious glance in Richard's direction before he redirected his glare onto the viscount.

"It's merely a harmless bet," Richard replied, waving a dismissive hand. "It's recorded in the betting book at White's. Has been for over a year."

"What *sort* of wager?" David repeated, this time slower and louder. Apparently, anxiousness was good at overcoming shyness, for at that moment, he didn't care who might hear the earl's answer.

"Uncle?" Marian whispered, her own brows furrowing before she glanced over at David with worry.

Marcus uncrossed his arms and leaned over the table as far as his belly would allow. "I bet him a hundred pounds you wouldn't be married before you were five-and-thirty," he admitted. "And Dicky here bet a hundred you *would* be married by then. "

"No names, you idiot," Richard whispered. "We're in the Soho Club."

Marcus directed a glare in the earl's direction. "Nothing is to be said by anyone beyond the club about what goes on here, so what's the problem?" he countered. "Besides, what the hell am I supposed to call you?"

Ignoring the query, Richard waved both his hands over the table. "Please sit down, you two. I'd rather we discuss this in private."

David held Marian's chair for her and then took the chair next to hers. Once he was settled, he felt for her hand under the table and pulled it into his own. He glanced over at her, dismayed to see her eyes were bright with unshed tears. "Since I am three-and-thirty years of age, you stand to collect one-hundred pounds if I marry your niece in the next year or so. I would like to do so within a..." He glanced over at her. "Within a month, if you're in agreement, my sweet."

"Oh, I would like that very much," Marian replied, a smile replacing the look of uncertainty that had appeared upon the revelation there was a wager involved.

Richard said, "Yes, yes, that would do nicely, except—"

"Not for me," Marcus protested.

The earl straightened in his chair. "So you'll owe me one hundred pounds," he said with a shrug, his eyes rolling before they settled on the viscount. "I've already won that much from you whilst playing whist today" he added with a shrug.

"Ninety-two quid is all," Marcus argued.

David's eyes rounded. "How many card games have you played?" he asked in alarm. "I was told to bring my pennies."

"And pennies will do you fine," Richard assured him.

"Pennies?" Marcus complained. "You told me to me we'd be playing for serious blunt," he claimed, directing an expression of annoyance on the earl.

"For when the two of us were playing, yes," Richard replied. "But not when the four of us are," he added, as if that should have alleviated any misunderstanding. The earl lifted his chin and said, "Now, where was I?"

"You said, 'yes, yes, that would do nicely, *except*'," Marian stated, imitating her uncle's delivery. "What's the exception?"

"Ah, yes. That would be the *timing* of a ceremony. Your father insisted a wedding be quick."

"How quick?" she asked, worry evident in her eyes.

"Within a week of accepting a proposal," Richard replied. "He thought it especially important you benefit from marrying with a special license."

Marian's eyes once again rounded. "But why?" she asked in dismay.

"It's fine, my sweet," David whispered, fairly sure he had more than enough money on his person to pay the fee. He pulled his chronometer from his waistcoat pocket. "How late is the ecclesiastical court at Doctors' Commons open? I believe I need to apply for a license at the Archbishop of Canterbury's office."

Richard's brows rose, as if he was impressed. "If you left in the next half-hour or so, you would make it," he replied.

About to rise, David paused when the earl waved his hand to indicate he should remain seated. He settled back in his chair but motioned for a footman. The servant hurried to his side and bent down. "Sir?"

"I am in need of my coach. Could you inform my driver?

He was going to pull into the mews around back," David explained.

"Right away, sir," the footman replied before he headed for the door.

Marian's bright eyes narrowed before she turned her gaze on her uncle. "I wasn't aware my father wished for a quick wedding," she commented.

"Sounds rather fishy to me," Marcus murmured, his scowl still in place.

"He was just looking out for you, darling," Richard commented. "Now... about the dowry—"

"You *do* have one for me," Marian said, her eyes still watery. "The solicitor assured me there was a dowry when he read my father's will."

Richard nodded. "There is a dowry, of course. Your father funded it long before he died," he assured her. "It's not much, though," he added with a grimace.

Up until that moment, David had completely forgotten that only the week before, he had thought of a dowry as a means to get by until the weather improved.

Had he subconsciously agreed to marry Miss Copper knowing he needed her dowry?

He gave his head a shake. Of course not. He hadn't given a thought to a dowry when he agreed to bc Marian's betrothed. But what had the earl been trying to say before the subject of a dowry had been raised? "Whatever it is will be fine," he stated. "But what did you mean when you said there might be... *conditions?*"

Richard's attention was on Marian when he said, "I must insist Miss Copper live in London. At least until she reaches her majority."

Although David was about to put voice to a protest, it was Marian who piped up and said, "But why?"

"Your father insisted," Richard stated, lifting a lanky shoulder. "He didn't want you relegated to the country estate whilst your husband was free to galavant in the capitol during the Season."

Well aware Marian had turned to stare at him, David kept his glare on Richard when he said, "As you are well aware, sir, I don't 'galavant' during the Season. Nor would I do so after I am wed."

"Well, *I* know that, but her father didn't know who she would be marrying," Richard reasoned.

"What did he consider her majority?" David asked, fearing the worst. Most young ladies were said to reach their majorities when they were five-and twenty while others had only to wait until they were one-and-twenty to collect their inheritances.

"As I recall, five-and-twenty."

David turned to Marian. "I know it's extremely impolite to ask a young lady her age, but might you share how old you are now, my sweet?"

"Oh, I don't mind at all," she said in a quiet voice. "I'll be three-and-twenty in a month."

Doing his best not to show his surprise—he had thought Marian might be far younger—David nodded. *Two years*, he thought as he struggled to keep an impassive expression on his face. They would have to live in the city for two years before he could take her to Engleston Park to live, at least when Parliament wasn't in session. He could abide it far better if he wasn't so damned shy. Living in the city meant he would be expected to attend certain entertainments. Spend a few nights a week at this club. Dance at balls.

"So... we'll simply live here in the capital until you're old enough," he stated. "I own a townhouse in Westminster." He winced when he remembered his mother still lived there. "Although it's nothing special."

"I'm sure it's fine," Marian replied, a prim grin replacing her look of worry. "Perhaps you could show it to me sometime during the next day or so. Mayhap give me a tour?"

"Of course. I was going to pay a call there anyway. We could go after my trip to the archbishop's office," he offered. "My... my mother still resides in the townhouse," he said as he winced.

"Oh?" Marian replied. "So she wasn't relegated to the country estate?" she asked, mimicking her uncle's words as she glared at Richard.

"She likes living in the city," David explained. "Her friends are here, and there's a coach and horses for her use."

Marian dipped her head. "I suppose she likes running her own household," she commented quietly.

David's eyes widened. "I'm quite sure she'd be happy to share the responsibility," he hedged. He hadn't even given a thought to how his mother would respond when told he was planning to marry. "That is, if you're of a mind to want to take on a household. And Engleston Park when we're in residence there." He glanced at Richard and Marcus, uncomfortable by how the earl seemed to hang on his every word while the viscount merely glared at him.

"Oh, very much," Marian assured him, her smile once again brightening her face.

Relieved, David turned his attention back to Richard. "Anything else before I acquire a marriage license?" he asked.

Richard regarded the three cards that were still face down in front of him. "Her father doesn't want her marrying a gambler."

Chuckling with relief, David let out the breath he'd been holding. "You know I am not," he stated. "And if that includes playing cards for pennies, then I shan't participate in the games you planned for today."

"That's not fair," Marcus stated. "How am I supposed to win back my blunt if we're not going to play for money?" he groused.

Ignoring the viscount, Richard reached an arm over the table, his hand held out. "Best wishes to you both," he stated as David shook his hand.

Glancing over at Marian, David gave her a brilliant smile. "Gentleman," he said as he turned his attention back to the earl and viscount. "If you'll excuse us, we'll be off to buy a license."

Marcus grumbled while Richard stood from his chair. "Don't be gone too long," he said. "The dinners here are especially good."

David exchanged a quick glance with Marian. "We should be back in time to change for dinner," he replied, offering her his arm.

The two took their leave of the card room. "I need to go up to my room for my redingote and a bonnet," Marian murmured.

"May I come with you?" David asked, glancing back toward the card parlor to see if they were being followed.

Marian's eyes rounded before a grin touched her lips. "Of course," she whispered.

CHAPTER 6
A COURTSHIP

t the top of the stairs
"I do hope you're not regretting anything," David murmured as they approached Marian's room.

She glanced over at him. "I am not. But I cannot help but think you will have second thoughts given my uncle's ridiculous conditions," she replied as she unlocked the door. David reached over and opened it for her.

"Other than the requirement to live in the city until you reach your majority, his conditions are to be expected," he said, his gaze taking in the room's decor. When he was in her bedchamber before, he hadn't even noticed it. All he remembered was Marian.

Kissing Marian.

"A special license is to be expected?" she queried before she noticed his attention wasn't on her. She sighed. "It's quite ridiculous, isn't it? All these shades of pink?" She waved a hand to indicate the cheval mirror standing in one corner. "The gold gilt?" she added with a scoff.

David merely shrugged before he turned his attention to his betrothed. "I believe the special license is meant to give your mother bragging rights." He paused, furrowing a brow. "Is... is your mother alive?"

Marian shook her head. "She died of influenza a few years ago. Not long after my father succumbed to it," she explained. "Which is why Uncle Richard is my guardian."

"I am sorry for your loss," David replied. "My father died of the flu ten years ago. A bit of a shock, really. I certainly wasn't expecting to inherit the barony before I was twenty-three years of age."

From the way her brows briefly crinkled, he knew she was sorting his age. "My condolences," she said in a quiet voice. "You were explaining the importance of a special license?" she prompted after a moment.

"Ah, yes. Well, it gives *you* bragging rights, I suppose," he replied. "And us the ability for us to choose when and where we wish to exchange vows without having to wait for the banns to be read," he added as he helped her into her coat. As a result, his fingers touched her shoulders, and for that briefest of moments, warmth and a fizzy sensation coursed through him. At first, he didn't think she noticed, but then he heard her slight inhalation of breath and wondered if she had felt the same. When her eyes darted to his and a knowing smile lifted the corners of her lips, he was sure.

"Will it shock people, do you suppose?" she asked as she reached for a bonnet resting on top of a dresser.

His mind still on the pleasant frissons he had experienced, David was caught off-guard by the query. "What do you mean?"

Marian inhaled softly. "Isn't it scandalous for two people to wed so quickly? Especially since... well, since we've only just met?" She rolled her eyes. "We haven't even been formally introduced."

David dipped his head. "Miss Marian Copper, may I have the honor of introducing myself?"

She grinned. "You have it, sir."

"I am David Morgan Engleston, the sixth Baron Engleston," he said as he bowed.

"I am very pleased to meet you, Lord Engleston," she said as she curtsied. David took her hand to his lips and kissed the back of it. When he straightened, he said, "You can call me David when we're in private like this," he whispered. "If you tire of calling me 'my dearest'."

"You can call me Marian if you tire of calling me 'my sweet'," she countered.

"I'll never tire of it," he whispered. He hesitated a moment, his gaze lowering to her lips. "May I kiss you?"

About to place the bonnet on her head, Marian lowered it and nodded. "I would like that very much. Whenever you are of a mind to do so."

Hesitating, David finally leaned down and touched his lips to hers. When he pulled away, he inhaled deeply. "I love the scent of you," he whispered.

Marian swallowed before she dipped her head. "Thank you. I thought it a bit of an extravagance, but my mother insisted," she said. "She had it created for me at Floris," she added, when David gave her a questioning glance. "When she thought I was going to have my come-out that year."

From the way she made the comment, David realized she referred to the year her mother had died. The requirements of mourning had obviously kept Marian from having a come-out.

"Ah, then they'll have the formula for when I buy more for you," he said as he offered his arm. "Shall we?"

Placing her hand on his arm, Marian allowed him to lead her down the stairs. David donned his greatcoat and hat and retrieved his umbrella on the way out of the building. As Marian was climbing into his coach, he said to Carver, "The archbishop's office in Doctors' Commons, and do try to hurry."

His driver blinked. "Yes, my lord."

"Might I sit next to you?" David asked as he stepped into the coach. He practically scoffed at hearing himself. His shyness wasn't in evidence when he was in the presence of Marian.

"I hoped you would," Marian replied as she settled into the velvet squabs in the direction of travel, pressing her body against the opposite wall from the door to give him more room. "This is quite nice. I've only ever seen leather interiors," she remarked.

David took the seat next to her, noticing how much space there was betwixt them. "You needn't feel as if you must sit so far away."

Giving him a tentative grin, Marian scootched a bit closer to him as the coach lurched into motion.

They sat in companionable silence for a few minutes before David asked, "Are you having second thoughts?"

Marian's eyes rounded. "No. No, I am not. But I cannot help but think we've been... set up," she said in a faraway voice.

"Set up?" he repeated. He turned to regard her. "What do you mean?"

"I promise. I didn't know anything about the wager. About my uncle winning money if you were to wed by a certain age," she explained.

"How could you?" David asked.

"But... when my uncle invited me to the Soho Club with him, he said I would be meeting my betrothed," she continued. "I thought he had arranged a marriage on my behalf, you see."

David gave a start. "Did he give you the name of this man to whom you were supposed to be betrothed?"

She shook her head. "That's why I..." She lifted a gloved hand and waved it from her lips to the reticule she clutched in the other. "Why I blurted out what I did when I first saw you," she explained. "And then, when you said you *were*, I was so..." She clamped her mouth shut as her face reddened.

A grin split David's lips before he suddenly sobered. "You were so... what?"

"*Relieved*," Marian said in a whisper. She swallowed. "I feared you would be an old fart..." She paused and inhaled sharply when she realized what she'd said, lifting a hand to cover her mouth.

A chuckle erupted from him. "That you don't think me an old fart is high praise, indeed," he replied before he leaned over and kissed her on the cheek. He would have kissed her on the lips, too, but the coach came to a stuttering halt. "We're already here," he murmured. "Would you like to come in with me?"

"Of course," she said at the same moment Carver opened the door, his dry hat an indication the rain had stopped falling.

David helped her down from the coach, and they proceeded into the four-story building.

A *half-hour later*
"Well, that wasn't difficult," David remarked, opening the coach door and helping Marian up the step. She gripped the license in her gloved hand as if it were a prized possession. "This is only the third one that has been issued this year," he added proudly.

"Would you tell me if I asked how much you had to pay for this?" Marian asked as she read the particulars.

Deciding it couldn't hurt to tell her, he said, "It was twenty-one pounds." Ignoring her gasp of shock, he added, "The real question is, do you wish to marry me today or wait until tomorrow?"

Although he hadn't given their wedding date much

thought when applying for the license, David certainly was now. If they married this afternoon—he had been given a card with the name and address of someone who would perform the ceremony before six o'clock—they would be spending this very night together as husband and wife. A wave of nervousness had him wondering if he had made a mistake in asking.

Marian's eyes rounded. "I suppose now is not the time to tell you I'm extremely shy and have no idea what I am supposed to do in the marriage bed," she blurted.

David blinked. He blinked again. Although he supposed he should have felt even more nervous by her claim, he instead felt relief. Profound relief. "Well, that makes two of us," he replied, chuckling softly. He turned to the driver, who had stepped down from the bench to help with the coach door.

"Where to, sir?" Carver asked.

"We're off to get married." He handed the driver the card he'd been given.

"Best wishes, sir," Carver said in awe, his gaze finally going to the pasteboard card. "But the... the address on this card is the same as the Soho Club, sir," he remarked, an expression of confusion crossing his face.

Thinking he might have mixed up the calling cards, David reached into his waistcoat pocket and pulled out the other card he possessed—the calling card he had used to enter the club. He glanced at the one his driver held, now sure he had given him the correct card. "Well, so it is. Let's stop at the townhouse, first, though. Miss Copper would like to see where she'll be living when we're in town for Parliament."

"Very good, sir." Carver held the door while David stepped into the coach.

Settling himself next to Marian, he glanced over at her to discover she was staring at him in disbelief. "What is it, my sweet?"

"I would never have guessed *you* were shy," she murmured.

He angled his head first one way and then the other. "I would not have guessed you were shy," he countered.

"It's why I never had a come-out. Well, besides the fact that I was in mourning when I was eighteen and then again when I was nineteen. Uncle offered to arrange a sponsor when I was twenty, but... I couldn't abide the thought of spending hours standing next to potted palms waiting for someone to ask me to dance," she explained.

"I admit I have been one of those gentlemen seeking refuge in the card room as a means of avoiding the dancing," David said. "So I suppose that explains why we've never met before today." He took one of her hands in his his. "Despite your shyness, why do you suppose you spoke to me first?"

"You weren't the old fart I was expecting, remember?" she teased. "Yet you didn't pause even one second to answer when I asked you if you were my betrothed."

He grinned as he nodded. "You... you emboldened me at that moment," he said. "You still had that effect on me when I was in the viscount's company a few minutes later. On the way to the card parlor, I admitted I was betrothed knowing he would react in shock, and he did," David claimed as he grinned at the memory. "I don't recall feeling so satisfied in all my life as I did at that moment he landed on his bum in the middle of a step and tore his breeches."

Marian gasped as a hand covered her mouth, her mirth evident in her eyes. "I felt the same way when I saw Uncle's expression the moment you kissed me on the cheek," she said as a brilliant smile lit her face. "He was so shocked." She slowly sobered as her gaze went to her mind's eye. "You don't really wish to live in town for the next two years," she murmured.

David hummed as he regarded her with an expression filled with mischief. "Oh, I won't mind if you're with me," he replied. "However, I think I might have an idea of how we can get 'round that particular requirement."

Marian's eyes rounded. "Oh? Do tell," she said, her good humor returning.

He held up a finger. "First, let's have you take a look at the place. Meet my mother. You might decide you like it enough that you'll wish to live there," he said.

"And if I *you* don't wish to live there?" she prompted.

Dipping his head, David said, "Well, I intend to take you on a wedding trip, of course." He delighted in hearing her inhalation of surprise. "There's no reason why it can't be a two-year trip. To my country house in Kent... or somewhere else," he added mischievously.

"You are a genius," she whispered happily.

An unfamiliar sensation of *something* filled his chest at hearing her comment. It wasn't pride, exactly. Or even satisfaction. But it did convince him he was making the right decision with regards to marrying Miss Marian Copper. "I think I've fallen in love with you," he said softly.

She squeezed his hand. "Well, that's a relief," she countered playfully. "I shouldn't wish to marry a man who wasn't falling in love with me."

The coach stopped, and from the jerk at the front, David knew Carver had stepped down from the bench. He glanced out the window, prepared to see Westminster at its winter worst.

Instead, he was pleasantly surprised.

The incessant rains seemed to have washed clean the rows of townhouses in his neighborhood. The pavement, still wet from the earlier rain, reflected the ray of sunshine that had split the clouds and was doing its best to warm the air.

"We're here," he said when he spotted the four-story Engleston townhouse beyond the window.

A wave of nervousness had him wishing they had simply

returned to the Soho Club, but David was determined his betrothed see what she would be living in when she married him.

If she married him.

CHAPTER 7
A TOUR IS A PRELUDE

moment later

Although he had feared the Engleston townhouse might appear shabby or soot-stained, David was pleasantly surprised to see that its smooth stucco exterior, made to look like some sort of Grecian marble, was neither. The black painted shutters were all plumb, and the cobalt blue door looked as new as the day it had been hung. A shiny brass mermaid knocker gleamed in the sunshine as did the brass kick plate at the door's base.

"This is *your* house?" Marian asked in awe.

"It is," he replied, although disbelief sounded in his words. He grinned when he noted her look of confusion. "If I expect the worst, then I can only be impressed when it is not," he said with a shrug. The nervousness he had felt only the moment before dissipated. First impressions were always the most important. Even if the interior was a wreck, at least the house appeared habitable from the outside.

Carver opened the coach door, and David stepped down to the pavement. He turned and offered Marian a hand, experimentally sniffing the air for the telltale odors of the nearby Thames and coal smoke. Instead, the air smelled fresh, as if the rain had simply washed away the stench, much as it had the soot.

Marian stood before the townhouse and glanced both left and right. "We must be near Westminster Abbey," she remarked.

"We are," David said. "It's only a few streets that way," he added, pointing with his umbrella. "I've been known to walk there when Parliament is in session." He took a deep breath and led her to the front door, rehearsing in his mind what he would tell his mother.

They hadn't even reached the green wrought iron gate when the front door opened to reveal the butler.

"Ah, Glover, it's good to see you again," David remarked as he held open the gate for Marian.

"And you, my lord," the butler replied as he stepped back and opened the door wider.

"Glover, this is my betrothed, Miss Marian Copper. Is my mother in residence?"

The butler bowed to Marian. "My lady," he said before turning his attention back to his master. "She is not, sir. She departed the city for Brighton two days ago. Said if she was to endure any more rain, she would do it there with her friends until either the end of August or until the rain quit," he explained. "Whichever came second. Her missive to you detailing her plans has probably not yet reached Engleston Park," he added as he took hats and coats from the couple.

"Oh, well I can't say I blame her," David remarked. "But I did wish to introduce her to Miss Copper." He allowed a shrug. "I shall at least give my sweet a tour of the house."

"I can have tea delivered to the parlor, sir. Should I have cook make a dinner for you two as well?"

David exchanged a quick glance with Marian. All his hastily made plans for that afternoon—the introduction to his mother, the tour of the house, and a wedding ceremony at the Soho Club before six o'clock—seemed to jumble in his mind. Perhaps his expression conveyed his confusion, for Marian squeezed his hand and said, "Yes. Tea in the parlor sounds perfect. Do have cook prepare a simple dinner for say... seven o'clock? The meal can be delivered to Lord Engleston's apartments. He will require his bedchamber this evening, of course, and might there be a bedchamber I could use starting tomorrow evening?"

Glover blinked. "Of course, my lady. I'll see to the tea right away," he said as he nodded, "and have the housekeeper see to the mistress suite."

"Oh, and do let the driver know his services won't be needed for the rest of the afternoon," Marian said as David stared at her in wonder.

"Yes, my lady."

The butler headed off through the front hall, his shoe heels clicking on the marble tile floor.

Marian watched him go before she turned to discover David still gazing at her. "What is it, my dearest?"

He swallowed. "You're very good at that," he remarked. "Making last-minute plans and running a household, I mean."

She grinned. "I do it every day at Penhurst Place," she said, referring to her uncle's London mansion. "I have been since I became his ward. He doesn't have a wife, nor do I expect he'll take another since he already has his heir."

David angled his head to one side, remembering the earl's son was away at university. "So... since you're having the driver dismissed for the afternoon, I take it we're not returning to the Soho Club until later this evening?" he asked in confusion.

Marian placed a hand on the top of his. "I think it's best we stay here for a time, don't you?" she replied as she surveyed the hall as if in awe. "We'll be so much more comfortable here."

"I do rather like the thought of dining in my apartment,"

he said, his nervousness returning. "Especially if I actually had an apartment and not merely a bedchamber."

Marian blinked, her happy expression momentarily faltering. "Does your bedchamber have a sitting area?"

David furrowed his brows. "I believe so. It's been some time since I was in there." At her look of confusion, he added, "I spend most of my time here in my study or in the library."

Her eyes rounded. "You have a library? Here?"

He nodded. "I do. And from your reaction, am I to conclude you are a reader?"

Hesitant to respond, Marian clasped her hands together. "Would you think less of me if I said yes?" she asked.

"I would think how fortunate I am to marry a woman with a brain," he replied in awe. His expression faltered. "I must warn you that although there is a decent collection of fiction—my mother is a reader of gothic novels—the majority of the tomes are rather dry. 'Modern Farming Techniques' and 'Animal Husbandry for the Gentleman Farmer' come to mind," he said on a wince.

Marian giggled. "Then I am sure to find something to read whilst you are engaged in the matters of your barony," she replied. "But I should warn you that my reading has included many works of non-fiction. Works that might be considered... *scandalous* for a woman of my age to have read."

David blinked. "Would these scandalous books be of French origin, by chance?"

A blush colored her cheeks before Marian dipped her head. "With color plates," she acknowledged.

David chuckled and then sobered. "I believe my library might include one or two of those books" he said before he cleared his throat. "Do you suppose there will enough time for tea and a tour before we must be back to the Soho Club to be wed?" he asked with worry as he pulled his chronometer from his waistcoat pocket. "'Tis already half-past four o'clock."

She grinned. "We do not, but who said anything about going back to the Soho Club this afternoon?" She arched a brow. "I should like to marry you on the morrow. After I've had the opportunity to purchase a suitable gown."

David couldn't help but hide his disappointment. "Oh. And... and in the meantime?" he stammered.

Marian stepped up to him and touched her lips to his. He immediately returned the kiss, his arms encircling her back as he pulled her hard against him. His fingers spread wide as they smoothed down to the small of her back, their tips following the bumps of her spine until it curved to the perfectly shaped globes of her bottom.

When he pulled away slightly, he touched his forehead to hers. "Why did you request a bedchamber for tomorrow night?" he asked in a whisper.

Marian glanced up at him through the curtains of her dark lashes. "I rather hoped I wouldn't require my own for this evening," she answered.

He swallowed. "Oh," he said on a breath. His eyes darted sideways. "Because...?"

She angled her head to one side. "Perhaps I was hoping for an invitation to yours," she murmured. "Especially since we'll be having our dinner there."

"Oh," he said with excitement. 'You have it, my sweet," he replied quickly. "Always. An open invitation."

Marian giggled again in an attempt to cover her nervousness. "Show me this house now, my dearest David, or we're going to be making love right here on the hall floor," she warned with a grin.

David chuckled, his smile widening as if he were imagining what she was suggesting. "My servants would all faint from shock," he murmured as he offered his arm.

"For a moment there, I thought *you* were going to," she said with a teasing grin.

"For a moment, I almost did," he claimed on a guffaw. "Now, where do I start?" He glanced around the hall.

Lined with caryatids featuring the busts of various Roman emperors and small statuary of Greek gods, the floor of the hall was tiled with alternating black and white marble squares. "This is the hall, where if you have enough servants, you can play chess," he said as he spread his arms. "Of course, we have to move the round table into this room first," he said as he led her into the breakfast parlor.

Although there was a sideboard along one long wall and four chairs lined up along another, there was no table in the middle. "I take it you don't have breakfast in here?" Marian asked as her brows crinkled.

"Only when we're playing chess," he replied with a wink. He quickly sobered. "I've had a table on order from Chippendale's studio for nearly two years," he said. "In the meantime, we've been eating breakfasts in the dining room."

"I'll have a word with Mr. Chippendale or one of his associates this week," Marian stated.

David blinked. "You will?"

She angled her head to one side. "Do you object?"

He shook his head. "Not at all," he replied, grinning as he led her to a small room that looked out on the front street. "The sitting room," he said. "Faces east, so it has the morning light and none of the afternoon heat."

Marian nodded approvingly before they moved to his study. "My haven," he said as he moved to the desk and thumbed through a small stack of correspondence on a silver salver. "We have invitations," he said as he popped the wax seal on one missive.

"Should I send our regrets?" Marian asked as she lifted one of the bright white notes and regarded the seal on the back with a critical eye.

"I rather imagine most of these have already taken place," he murmured as he read an invitation to a ball that had occurred in April.

"I'll see to the appropriate responses," she said as she opened an invitation to a garden party. "When do you suppose we will be departing for Engleston Park?"

David glanced up from a letter he was reading. "I suppose that depends on when you'd like to begin our wedding trip," he hedged.

"Then I shall send regrets for all of these," she replied with a grin.

"I do like the way you think," he said as he tossed the letter he'd been reading onto the desk. "On to the dining room," he said as he headed for the door.

Marian hesitated but followed the baron to the next room off of the main hall. Although it featured a table that might seat ten or twelve, the dining room was huge by townhouse standards. "We could host a ball in here," she murmured in awe.

"Oh, please. Let's not," David countered.

She giggled at the very moment Glover appeared on the threshold to announce tea had been served in the parlor.

"Upstairs," David said before Marian could ask where the parlor was located. He offered an arm, and the two climbed the flight of stairs located on one side of the main hall. "It's not particularly grand, I know," he said as they made their way.

"But it provides a rather glorious vantage," she said as they looked over the railing to the hall below.

"The parlor is right here," he said in a quiet voice, his head nodding to a set of open double doors.

"How convenient for our guests," she replied, glancing between the top of the stairs and the parlor.

David regarded her with a grin. "You're being a very good sport about this," he said in a quiet voice.

Marian gave a start. "Why do you say that?"

He shrugged. "You've been running the household at Penhurst Place for... for how long?" They headed into the parlor.

"A few years," she admitted.

"This must seem... petty," he said with a wince. A quick glance around the parlor had him pleasantly surprised, though. It appeared brighter and fresher than he remembered, and there was a pleasant scent of pine in the air.

Marian shook her head. "Not at all. I've never thought of Penhurst Place as my own. As if I would ever truly be the lady of the house," she amended. "At any moment, Uncle Richard can take a wife, and I will be relegated to a guest bedchamber at the end of a long forgotten corridor."

David gave a start. "I promise that as my wife, that shall never happen to you," he whispered.

Her eyes suddenly narrowed. "Do you suppose...?" She didn't complete the thought out loud. Had her uncle decided to remarry? Did he already have someone in mind to become the new Lady Penhurst?

Coming to the same conclusion, David furrowed a brow and pulled her into his arms. "If Lord Penhurst is intending to remarry, he has said nothing to me," he murmured. "He already has an heir."

"Cousin William," she acknowledged, her curt response suggesting she didn't care for the young man.

"Perhaps Penhurst really did plan for us to meet. See you settled," David suggested. He shrugged. "If that's the case, his plan is working to perfection."

She dipped her head. "I do hope you're not feeling as if he has manipulated the situation somehow. Because... because I do," she admitted.

David winced. "Are you having second thoughts?"

Her eyes rounded. "Oh, not about us," she assured him.

"But I have every intention of thoroughly scolding him when next I see him."

Chuckling at the thought of Marian Copper giving the Earl of Penhurst the what-for, David remembered something. "Careful, my sweet," he said, about to remind her that Penhurst controlled her dowry. "Best to keep him in our good graces since we'll be eloping soon."

Marian inhaled softly. "Of course." She glanced around the parlor. "Well, this is certainly cozy. Not the least bit shabby," she remarked. "Penhurst Place's parlor is well-used," she added with a wince.

"I hope you'll like the country house," David said in a quiet voice. "That you'll make it your own. That you'll want to stay there with me for the rest of our lives," he added before he lowered his lips to hers and kissed her quite thoroughly.

When they came up for air, Marian stared at him for a moment before she inhaled softly. For the first time since they had met, she was sure she felt the evidence of his arousal behind the placket of his breeches. Her eyes darted down to confirm her suspicion. "Our tea will be growing cold," she whispered.

He swallowed. "Indeed," he replied, his face reddening with his embarrassment.

"A quick cup and we'll head upstairs to your bedchamber," she suggested.

"We will?

"Or... we can simply skip the tea," she went on, ignoring his query.

"I'll just grab the biscuits," David said as he plucked the plate of biscuits from the tray and returned to the threshold. "I don't know about you, but I'm starving, and I have reason to believe I'll require sustenance for what is about to happen."

Marian displayed a prim grin. "I'll bring the tea," she

offered as she lifted the salver from the low table in front of a rose velvet settee. "I don't know about you, but I'm rather thirsty."

David watched as she approached him, carrying the tray as if she'd done it a thousand times. Perhaps she had. "If I haven't told you already, I find you rather gorgeous," he blurted.

Marian blinked before she allowed a brilliant smile. "If you're thinking to ply me with compliments to entice me into your bed, then you should know that your plan is working to perfection," she said.

His mouth opening and closing much like a fish, David attempted a response before he realized she was giving him a compliment of sorts. "This way," he said as he led her to the next flight of stairs, this one located on the opposite wall from the first. "My mother took this room since it faces east," he explained when they had reached the top of the stairs. "My... *apartment*," he said in a teasing voice. "And the mistress suite are back here," he added as he indicated the floor's only corridor. "As well as a guest bedchamber and a bathing chamber."

"And the third floor?" she prompted as she glanced about for evidence of another flight of stairs.

"Servants' quarters and if I remember correctly, a nursery," he murmured. "They can be reached using the servants' stairs there in the corner."

"A very efficient floor plan," she remarked as he paused before the last door along the corridor. Holding the plate of biscuits in one hand while he used his other to push the door handle, David hesitated before opening the door.

"Please know that I did not plan for this to happen," he said, finally leaning against the wood panel until his bedchamber was revealed.

"How could you?" Marian countered, sweeping into the room. "Unless you knew something I didn't know." She headed directly to the low table in front of the fireplace and set the tea tray on it. She went about preparing cups for tea, impressed that Glover had seen to lighting several lumps of coal in the fireplace. With all the drapes pulled shut against the chill, the meager flame provided enough light by which to see.

About to mention his growing suspicion about the Earl of Penhurst's intentions for the two of them, David decided it best he simply enjoy the results. He was betrothed. He was aroused. And he was about to share a bed with a woman for the very first time in his life.

CHAPTER 8
TEA BEGETS A TUMBLE

"How do you take your tea?" Marian asked.

"A bit of milk is all," David answered, joining her in front of the fireplace. He set down the plate he'd been holding next to the tea tray and helped himself to a lemon biscuit. Finishing it off in two bites, he went for another as Marian offered him a cup of tea. "Thank you," he said. His gaze landed on the mantel clock when it began to chime.

Five o'clock.

By the time dinner was brought up at seven, he would be a thoroughly ruined man. But then, Marian would be a thoroughly ruined woman. There would be no choice for her but to marry him.

That last thought didn't provide the sort of comfort he was seeking just then. That they were doing the right thing.

But she didn't seem the least bit concerned with her new future. If anything, she seemed more committed to their marriage than she had any right to be.

Did betrothals always cause this sort of double-guessing? Questioning what was right versus what was best? Was a marriage to him Marian's best option? Was *she* his best option?

Well, she was his only option. Now that they had kissed one another so many times, David couldn't imagine doing so with anyone else. As for what they were about to do, they were on equal footing. Both virgins. Both about to give themselves to one another in an ancient act that had seen to the survival of mankind for thousands of years. He'd be damned if he didn't do his part.

Besides, he needed an heir.

David ate the second biscuit and then drained his tea in two swallows.

Noting his anxiousness, Marian finished her first cup of tea and stood. "You looked terribly fierce just then," she said, her voice suggesting she was impressed.

His resolve faltering, David dipped his head. "I didn't mean to frighten you," he said.

Moving to stand in front of him, she offered a hand to help him stand. "Oh, I'm not frightened," she replied. "But I am intrigued by what thoughts caused it."

David stared at her bare hand for a moment before his eyes widened. "I didn't give you a ring," he said, coming to his feet.

Before Marian could say anything in response, he made his way to the tall dresser on the long wall. Opening a walnut jewel box, he plucked a gold band from its velvet lining and held it up in the dim light. Apparently not satisfied, he used a finger to push around the other items inside the box before extracting another ring. "Ah, finally," he said with relief as he regarded the jeweled ring in the palm of his hand.

Marian glanced over his shoulder. "It's very beautiful," she murmured.

He turned and captured her right hand in his. "I'm glad you like it, because this one is your betrothal ring," he said as he slid the gold and gemstone ring onto her fourth finger.

"And this one," he retrieved the gold ring from the top of the dresser, "is your wedding band." He slid it onto her left ring finger.

When he glanced up, he found Marian staring at her hands in awe. "They're gorgeous," she whispered. "Truly. How is it you have them?"

David felt relief. "Well, this one was my grandmother's," he said as he pointed to the ruby ring. "And this was my great-grandmother's," he added as he held up her left hand. "I suppose I should propose, don't you suppose?"

Marian blinked. "I suppose," she replied on a titter.

"Will you marry me?"

Marian blinked. "Yes. Yes, I'll marry you," she replied happily before she lifted her face to kiss him.

As their lips met, her fingers went to work on the fastenings of his topcoat, undoing the three jet buttons. Before they had finished the next kiss, she had his waistcoat open. She was in the middle of undoing the buttons on the placket of his breeches when he covered her hand with his.

"Boots first," he whispered as he struggled to catch his breath. He cursed himself for wearing boots instead of shoes that day, but he was reminded that he had started this rainy day traveling in a coach.

Had that been only this morning?

He doffed his topcoat and waistcoat as Marian undid the knot of his cravat. "You make an excellent valet," he remarked.

"Why, thank you, sir," she replied. Marian stepped back and turned around. "Now we'll see how you do as a lady's maid," she teased.

David froze. "What... what do I do?" he stammered.

Turning her head so her chin rested on her shoulder, she said, "You can start by undoing the buttons down my back," she instructed.

His fingers fumbling for a moment, David did her bidding

until the bodice of the yellow gown separated and fell forward.

"Uh…"

"Now untie the stays," she said quietly.

"Uh… there are a number of ties back here," he mumbled.

"Undo them all."

"All?"

She tittered as she once again rested her chin on her shoulder. "Just pull the tie of each bow and use your fingers to loosen the strings." She felt his fingers touch the bare skin above her chemise, and she shivered. "That tickles," she whispered.

Emboldened, David leaned down and placed a kiss on the same spot. Marian inhaled softly and closed her eyes when he turned and placed his lips on her cheek. "I'll have to redo all these ties later, won't I?" he asked.

She shrugged, which had the bodice falling completely from her torso and the sleeves from her arms. Wiggling her hips, the gown dropped to the floor. "Not until the morning," she replied.

His fingers once again pressed into her underclothes. "We're not going back to the Soho Club tonight, are we?"

Marian turned around. "I certainly hope not," she replied. "Unless you prefer being surrounded by pink." When she saw his look of confusion, she said, "My room there? Yours is located next to the viscount's, and I shouldn't wish for him to hear us whilst we're in the… in the throes of passion."

David blinked and swallowed. "Oh, I should hope not. He's already sore with me over our betrothal. I would hate to make him jealous, too."

Grinning, Marian turned so her back was once again facing the baron.

He swallowed. "Won't your uncle be expecting us, though?"

"Possibly, but... we did leave to acquire a license," she reminded him. "He'll think we've married and are spending the night here. You did mention you were going to show me the townhouse."

"I did," David remembered, relaxing somewhat. For a moment, he had imagined Bow Street Runners combing the city for them, believing he had kidnapped the young lady. "I did," he said more forcefully as he plucked all the ties before him.

Two petticoats and a set of stays fell to the floor.

"Oh, my," he whispered when he realized she was left wearing only her short chemise and stockings.

"My turn," she said as she faced him and began unwrapping the ends of the silk cravat from around his neck. She carefully folded it in half and draped it over the back of a chair. Grasping handfuls of his shirt, she pulled it up and over his head.

For a moment, time seemed to stop. As if she couldn't decide whether or not to stare at the expanse of his bare chest or his arms or concentrate on his face.

Once again emboldened, David lifted a hand to her jaw and held her head as he bestowed a kiss on her lips. "I'm going to remove my boots now," he said.

She swallowed. "I'll see to turning down the bed linens," she said before she turned and headed for the bed.

Leaning against one of the chairs so he could remove his boots, David watched as she leaned over the edge of the bed and saw to folding back the counterpane and linens to the end of the mattress. The entire time, her bare bottom was on display, her upturned quim peeking out from between the tops of her thighs as if in invitation.

Gulping, David pulled first one boot and then the other from his feet, his attention on Marian's bottom the entire time. As he watched, his cock lengthened and hardened, straining against his breeches until he was forced to push them down along with his smalls. He had his stockings off only the moment before she completed her task and turned to face him.

This time she didn't avoid staring, a small smile finally appearing before she moved closer to him. She reached out with a hand and touched the dark hairs that dusted his chest near a nipple.

He flinched at her touch, but didn't pull away. Instead, he placed his hands at her hips, more to steady himself as he pushed away from the chair to stand straighter.

"Will you help me with my stockings?" she asked as she trailed her fingertips down the front of his body until her forefinger slid through the dark curls above his manhood.

"Of course," he said as he watched two of her fingers trace a vein along his erection. He struggled to breathe. "But if you keep that up, I shan't have anything left for you."

"Oh," she said as she jerked her hand away.

David immediately regretted his words. "I like the way you touch me," he whispered, lifting her hand so he could kiss her fingertips. His other hand slid around her hip to the globe of her bottom, smoothing over the silken skin to pull her against him until his manhood was pressed into her belly.

"Perhaps we can leave my stockings on for now," she whispered, crossing her arms to grab the fabric of her chemise until she had it over her head and off of her body. She tossed the garment onto the pool of fabric that had already been formed by her gown and underthings.

David swallowed at briefly seeing her bare breasts before they were pressed against his chest. Kissing her hard, he groaned as he used both hands to lift her by her bottom. "Hold on," he managed to say before he carried her to the bed.

Marian wrapped her legs around his thighs for the quick trip, suppressing a yelp when he managed to get both her and him onto the bed.

"How do I pleasure you?" he asked when he had her positioned beneath him, his attention on her breasts.

"I'm not exactly... Oh!" she responded at the same moment his mouth descended on one nipple. She inhaled sharply as he suckled. Inhaled again when a hand cupped the other breast, molding it in the palm of his hand. "Like that, I suppose," she said as she exhaled on a half-giggle.

He moved his mouth to her other breast and slid a hand down the front of her body and over her mound. He gave up his hold on her breast, his lips trailing down her chest and belly while the tip of his middle finger slid through the folds protecting her womanhood. "Will you spread your legs for me, my sweet?" he whispered.

She did so, lifting a knee slightly. He felt her damps curls, felt the honeyed folds, and gently pressed where he thought her opening might be. When she bucked beneath him, her soft cry startling him, he froze. "Did I hurt you?" he asked in confusion.

"Hardly," she breathed. "Do it again if you'd like."

Intrigued, he circled the area that had her reacting before, his finger drenched with her ambrosia as he sought what he hoped was the source of her pleasure. He added his forefinger to the quest, relieved to hear her soft cries of 'yes' over and over again until one of her hands covered his. "I'm ready for you," she whispered.

Lifting his body over hers, David felt relief when her hand gripped his cock and placed it at her opening. Although he would have liked a bit more direction, he understood when the tip of his manhood disappeared.

Marian lifted her knees higher. "Push harder, my dearest," she whispered.

"I don't want to hurt you," he argued, but all at once, his cock seemed to find its bearings and bury itself into her. He growled at the sudden sensation of warmth and tightness that surrounded his manhood. At the feeling of the silk of her stockings sliding along his thighs as Marian pinned him with her knees. At the tickle of her nipples against his chest. At the pricks of her fingernails leaving half-moon dents in his back as she gripped him.

He stared down at her, surprised by her serene expression. "I think I have died and gone to heaven," he whispered.

She grinned. "Not yet, you haven't," she murmured.

"Are you... all right?"

Nodding her head in the pillow, she seemed to think on his query a moment before she said, "It feels as if you've filled me up and there is no more room inside."

"Does it hurt?"

"Not anymore. You can... you can move now."

David furrowed a brow before he realized what she meant. "Of course." He pulled himself nearly all the way out of her before he pushed again, grinning when he felt her quim lift to meet his gentle thrust. From there, he understood what to do, pulling out and thrusting into her over and over until he knew his climax was imminent. Stars danced before his eyes as intense pleasure took him from the here and now and left him suspended over her, his arms taut and his neck straining as his head lifted, and he squeezed his eyes shut.

He might have remained like that for a few seconds or a few minutes, but it was Marian who finally pulled him back to reality. To the pillow next to her head. Wrapping her arms around his back in an effort to keep him from falling off of her body. Kissing the space between his brows as he sighed.

"I do believe this is the very best betrothal I could ever hope for," David murmured. He buried his head into the pillow above her shoulder, his nose pressed into the space behind her ear.

Marian slowly lowered her knees along his thighs even as she tightened her hold on him with her arms. When her toes touched the mattress, she took first one experimental breath and then another. With his chest pressed onto hers, she could feel his heartbeats warring with her own until they seemed to merge into one as he dozed.

He had filled her first with his manhood and then with a warmth that seemed to permeate throughout her entire body. The little darts of pleasures still danced about beneath her skin. Prickles of heat where their bodies were joined had her clenching on him, each contraction eliciting tremors in his body and a matching inhalation of breath she could clearly hear as well as feel.

One of his hands smoothed over her shoulder and down the side of her torso, a thumb pressing into the side of her breast where it was mounded against his chest.

The sensation might have been merely a tickle, but Marian inhaled sharply as his touch set off a series of frissons beneath her skin. She clenched on him again as a grin touched her lips. Her eyes rounded. "Are you all right?" she asked in a worried whisper.

He chuckled. "I am far better than all right," he murmured, lifting his head enough to kiss the corner of her mouth. "In fact, I can hardly wait to do that again."

She grinned.

"How long must I wait?" His eyes widened. "Oh, that's terribly selfish of me," he said. "Are you hurt? Are you sore? Are you ready to throw me out of the bed?"

"Hardly," she replied, grinning.

When his brows furrowed, she regarded him with worry. "What is it?"

"Are you all right? Did I hurt you?" he asked again, moving to support himself on one elbow.

"I am fine," she replied. "I felt nothing more than a pinch," she added when he didn't look convinced. "Although I do feel as if I'm not all here," she whispered, lifting her chin so her head was forced deeper into the pillow.

"Oh, you're here," he murmured happily. "I've got you. But I think I know what you mean," he added in a faraway voice. "You're in bits and pieces and floating about." His fingers lifted to wiggle in the air above her shoulder.

She gave a start. "Yes, that's it," she whispered. "You feel like that, too?"

He kissed the space behind her ear. "Since the moment I met you." At the sound of her scoff, he added, "But more so in these last few minutes." He raised his head from the pillow to place a series of kisses along her jaw and then onto her lips. "And here I am practically suffocating you," he said as he attempted to move more of his body off of hers.

"I look forward to when we can do it again, but I think perhaps we should wait until after dinner. You'll need your strength," she teased.

He chuckled. "I like the way you think," he said before he kissed the top of her breast and attempted to roll off her body.

Marian held onto him, her arms tightening around his back. "Don't go," she said.

He relaxed back into her hold. "If you're sure. It's just... I'm suddenly feeling very tired. I fear I'm going to fall asleep."

Tittering, Marian inhaled and let the breath out on a sigh of satisfaction. "Then do so," she replied. "I'm not going anywhere." Reaching for the counterpane, she lifted the edge up and over him. "But I rather imagine your backside is growing cold."

"I wouldn't notice if it was," he whispered. "But thank you," he said before he fell asleep.

Marian's lips lifted in a grin as she wondered how he

could be so sleepy when her entire body seemed more alive than she could ever remember. Before she could think too long on it, she too was sound asleep.

They didn't awaken until the mantel clock chimed seven times.

CHAPTER 9
A DINNER AND CONVERSATION

*S*even o'clock

"Do you have an extra wrapper I might wear?" Marian asked when she was aware of footsteps coming down the corridor.

David blinked several times. "Wrapper?" he repeated.

"A dressing robe? A banyan?" she clarified.

"Oh," he said as he was suddenly up and out of the bed, unaware Marian watched him. Although she had seen the front of him naked earlier that evening, she hadn't seen his backside. From her vantage in the bed, she studied how his muscles moved beneath his skin, how his thighs and calves worked. A pleasant tremor passed beneath her skin, and she marveled at the thought she might experience such a sensation every time she saw him unclothed.

He disappeared through a door in the corner and emerged with a silk dressing robe. "Like this?"

A firm knock sounded at the main door to the bedchamber. "I'll get it," he said as he pulled the robe on and Marian dived under the covers.

"Your dinner, sir," Glover said as he held a tray laden with two covered plates, various utensils, a bottle of wine and two glasses.

"Ah, right over here in front of the fireplace," David said, waving to where the tea service was still set up. "You can take that, but leave the biscuits if you would."

"Of course, sir. Will there be anything else?" The butler kept his attention on his master, deliberately ignoring the lump in the bed.

"Breakfast in the morning," David stated. "Eight o'clock. Do bring a cup of chocolate and... make sure the driver is ready to depart by nine. We'll be going shopping before we head back to the Soho Club."

"About that, sir..." Glover started to say.

"What is it?" David asked, noting the servant's curious expression.

"A footman arrived from there a few minutes ago. Something about Miss Copper having gone missing? I had him wait in the front salon."

David blinked. "Miss Copper isn't missing," he replied. "Nor is she Miss Copper any longer," he added, feeling emboldened. "She is Lady Engleston."

"Yes, sir." Glover looked uncertain for a moment. "Should I send the footman with any other message?"

Sighing, David considered how to respond. "If the Earl of Penhurst is interested in being a witness, we'll have a formal wedding ceremony at the Soho Club at eleven in the morning. Then we'll be off on our wedding trip the day after," he said, deciding he rather liked the hastily made plan. It would allow him to take Marian to his house in the country.

"Have a footman sent to Penhurst Place with the message that Lady Engleston's maid is to pack a trunk or two and be ready to join us for the trip," he added, rather enjoying the growing look of shock Glover was displaying. "Oh, and have the Soho Club footman tell Lord Penhurst I expect Lady Engleston's dowry to be deposited into my account at Barclay's within the week. I need to set up a generous settlement for her and our children when I next see my solicitor."

Glover listened intently before he gave a nod. "Yes, sir. Very good, sir."

The butler took his leave and David shut the door. He turned to discover Marian sitting up in the bed, the linens pulled up to hide her nakedness. The knot atop her head, which had been smooth and in perfect condition upon their arrival earlier that afternoon, was now a messy bun that somehow made her even more beautiful than he remembered.

"Lady Engleston?" she said in a teasing voice. "I thought your butler was going to faint."

"He's your butler, too," David said as he moved to the edge of the bed. "My baroness."

Marian sat up straighter, one of her hands going to her hair before she winced. "I'm quite sure I must look a fright."

"You're gorgeous like that," he said, smiling.

Marian displayed an expression of disbelief before she slowly grinned. "Says the man who has decided he likes making love and wishes to do it again?" she guessed.

He nodded. "I'll not deny it, but I do require sustenance. I'm starving," he claimed. "Will you join me for dinner?" he asked, waving to the tray of plates.

"Do you have an extra robe?"

His eyes widened. "Oh. Yes. Yes, I believe I do," he said as he once again disappeared into the dressing room. He emerged with a heavy velvet banyan and helped her into it.

"What would you have done if I didn't have an extra one?" he asked.

She gave him a quelling glance. "I suppose I would have had to eat dinner naked," she replied, grinning when David's expression faltered. "Oh, please don't regret finding it," she quickly added. "We would have had to eat dinner in bed."

"I wouldn't have minded," David remarked.

Marian saw to removing the covers from their plates while David poured the wine. "I've never eaten a meal like this," she said as she pulled one of the plates to her lap. "But I've always wanted to."

He grinned as he set a glass on the table for her. "Sort of an indoor picnic," he murmured, helping himself to the other plate. Instead of sitting in the upholstered chair opposite her, he lowered himself to the floor, his back against the chair. "To us," he said, lifting his wine glass from the table.

"To us," she replied, copying his move. She regarded the manner in which he lounged as he held his plate in one hand and his fork in the other. One leg was crossed over the other, his bare feet poking out from beneath the hem of his robe. "You've done this before," she accused.

He grinned. "Not in this house, I haven't," he claimed. "But I admit to having eaten whilst sitting on the floor of my study in Engleston Park."

She regarded him with a look of surprise. "Is the floor especially comfortable there?"

Chuckling, he said, "Not particularly. But it's warm by the hearth, and if my dog is there to lay on my feet..." He shrugged.

"You have a dog? One you allow indoors?" she asked, her forkful of peas stopped in mid-air.

For a moment, David wondered if he had erred in mentioning the sheepdog. "I do. Mr. Scot is very well behaved and quite the master of keeping my feet warm whilst I sit at my desk," he explained.

"Mr. Scot?" she repeated with a grin. "You named your dog Mr. Scot? Is there a Mrs. Scot?"

"There is not, and I wasn't the one who named him. One of the servants did. When he showed up at the back door carrying a half-dead pheasant and acting like he owned the place. He just walked in, dropped the bird at her feet, and made himself comfortable under my desk."

"He sounds delightful," Marian remarked.

"I hope you like him. He'll love you."

Marian finished a bite of roast beef. "I'm sure I will," she murmured.

"God, I hope you don't regret this," David blurted, setting aside his plate as his brows furrowed in worry.

Lowering her plate to the table and then joining him on the floor, Marian sat next to him and placed her head against his shoulder. "I know you don't believe me now, but... I won't," she whispered. "I will admit... I wondered if *you* will regret it?"

His eyes widened. "Never," he said, running one of his hands over his head, his fingers spearing his hair so it was left with furrows.

Marian lifted a hand and smoothed his hair, watching as he closed his eyes and sighed.

"I've never met anyone like you." He turned his head to regard her with a wan grin. "I've always been too shy. Too afraid of meeting new people," he claimed. "I think we're good together," he added, although the sound of a question was apparent in his voice.

"Oh, we are," she assured him. "I could not have asked for a better lover."

"Ah, I think you could have," he argued. "But I'm glad you didn't." He dipped his head, a look of sadness crossing his face. "Do you really intend to sleep in the mistress suite?"

Marian furrowed a brow. "Not if I'm welcome in here."

David's eyes widened. "Then why did you ask for the mistress suite to be prepared?"

She grinned but didn't answer, allowing him to come to his own conclusion.

"You needn't wait for an invitation from me," he said. "I

adore having you in bed with me. I don't think I've slept so well in all my life. All warm and... *warm*," he murmured. "And you make an excellent pillow."

"I am happy to hear it," she whispered. "I shall endeavor to be the best pillow I can be every night." After a pause, she added, "As for the mistress suite—"

"I understand you would want a place for your clothes. For your things," he reasoned.

Marian leaned over and kissed him on the cheek. "I can already tell you are going to make the very best husband."

He wrapped an arm around her shoulder and pulled her onto his lap. Kissing her for several minutes, he finally pulled away to regard her with a look of uncertainty. "Is there a chance you might like to return to the bed?"

She tittered. "So we can continue our conversation there?"

David screwed up his face in a grimace. "I had something else in mind..." Before he could even finish his response, Marian was up and headed toward the bed, the banyan landing on the end of the mattress before she paused to slip under the covers.

"Are you coming?"

Chuckling, David said, "In more ways than one." He was up and off the floor and onto the bed in only a few seconds as Marian giggled in delight.

CHAPTER 10
A DAY OF RECKONING

The following morning

The heavens had apparently decided they favored David Engleston's new life. At least, that's what he thought when he awoke at dawn to discover the skies were clear.

After kissing his wife to wakefulness and enjoying a morning tumble, he rang for a bath. They ate their breakfast in bed, and after a rather raucous time in the tub—he was sure there was more water on the floor than in the tub when they finished—he helped Marian into her clothes.

About to don the same clothes he had worn the day before, he remembered he had formal attire in his dressing room. "What color gown will I be buying for you today?" he asked as he selected a top coat and dark breeches.

"You won't be buying my gown," Marian replied as she pulled a stocking onto her leg. "I intend to have it put on my uncle's account."

David watched as her leg disappeared into the knit fabric, the oddest sensation making him wonder if he would always react the same whenever he saw her naked limbs.

He hoped so.

"Does he know that?" he asked.

Marian giggled as she tied the ribbon at the top of the stocking. "He won't even notice," she murmured. "His man of business pays his bills. As for color... why do you ask?"

David stuffed his shirt into his breeches. "I thought to wear the same color waistcoat."

Halting in the middle of pulling on her other stocking, Marian regarded him with a grin. "Do you have a yellow one?"

Disappearing into the dressing room for a moment, David emerged with a pale yellow satin waistcoat embroidered with birds and leaves. He held it up. "It's the only yellow one I possess."

"It's perfect," she said as she finished tying the ribbon of the stocking. She made her way to stand before him and helped with his cravat as he saw to buttoning his coats.

Then they were off, her arm on his as they made their way down the stairs, out of the house, and into the coach. The trip to Suzanne's in Oxford Street was quick. David was offered a cup of tea whilst Marian disappeared into a dressing room. When she emerged a few minutes later, wearing a pale yellow gown sprigged with birds and leaves, David nearly spilled his tea.

"How...?" he sputtered, glancing down at his waistcoat.

"Birds and leaves are fashionable," the modiste remarked. "Shall I wrap it up for you?"

"Thank you, but no. I'll be wearing it for my wedding today," Marian replied.

"Then I shall wrap up your other gown," Suzanne offered. "And best wishes to you both."

Amazed the visit to the modiste hadn't taken even an hour, David was helping Marian into the coach when he spotted a florist shop. "I'll be only a moment," he said as he hurried off. He returned with a bundle of hothouse daffodils and tulips.

"They're gorgeous," Marian whispered as he offered her the beribboned bouquet.

"Not as gorgeous as you are," he replied. The coach jerked into motion, and all at once, nervousness had David struggling to breathe.

"What is it?" Marian asked, her nose hidden by the yellow and red blooms.

"I hope your uncle doesn't plant a facer on me when we arrive at the Soho Club," he said.

Marian tittered. "He won't. I promise," she replied. "He might... scold you. Probably scold me," she added with a grin. "But if the footman relayed your message correctly, then he can't say he wasn't warned."

"Let's hope Viscount Huntley isn't still smarting over his wager with your uncle," David remarked.

Marian's happy expression faltered at the reminder of the wager. "Huntley is a petty man," she murmured. "I don't know why Uncle spends any time in his company."

David gave a start at hearing the rebuke in her voice. "Haven't they been friends for a long time?"

She shrugged. "I suppose."

Concerned over her sudden change in mood—she had been so happy until the mention of the viscount—David angled his body so he could better see her face. "What's happened?"

Marian dipped her head so her nose ended up in the bouquet. She inhaled deeply before she lifted her face. "He proposed marriage. Several years ago," she said.

"To you?" David asked in alarm.

She gave him a quelling glance.

"Oh, I apologize. I didn't mean that the way it sounded," David said as his eyes widened. "I just meant... I wasn't aware... well, I didn't realize he wasn't already married," he said lamely.

"He's a widower," she explained. "Thought he was doing

me—or Uncle, maybe—a favor. I told him I would think on it." She lifted her shoulder in a shrug. "I didn't really need to think on it. I knew I did not wish to marry him, so I gave him my answer the next time I saw him."

"Thank you for turning down his offer," David said, placing a hand over hers.

She gave him a wan grin. "I think he's still sore at me. But I told Uncle I couldn't marry him. He's old enough to be my father, and I didn't wish to be part of a marriage of convenience."

"I cannot blame you," David replied. "Besides, he's a bit of a toad. You're much better off with me."

Marian giggled. "I already know I am," she murmured as the coach came to a halt in front of the club.

Pulling the Soho Club cards from his waistcoat pocket—one for entry and the one for the person who could marry them—David offered his arm as they made their way along the pavement to the club's door. The footman had it opened before David had a chance to show his card.

"Might you know where I could find the person who performs the wedding ceremonies?" David asked.

The footman regarded the calling card a moment and a grin lightened his face. "Mrs. Skarsgard will see to the arrangements. Have you a license?"

"Indeed," David replied, patting his topcoat. He had stuffed the document into a hidden pocket that morning, worried it might be lost otherwise.

"She'll take care of the particulars and see to it you two are married by noon. Be sure to stay for the breakfast before you head off."

Marian and David exchanged quick glances, deciding they wouldn't mention they would be keeping their rooms for another night at the club. If the footman from the night before had relayed David's instructions, then Marian's lady's maid would have her clothes packed and ready for her to depart for Engleston Park the next morning.

They gave their coats and hats to the club's butler and made their way up the stairs to Mrs. Skarsgard's office.

"Ah, you'll be needing our wedding services," she said before David had a chance to tell her why they were there.

"You already know?" Marian asked.

The proprietress motioned to the bouquet of flowers Marian held. "New gown, flowers, matching waistcoat..." she replied with a shrug. "The chapel is ready, and the priest will join you there in a half-hour."

"Chapel?" David repeated.

"Downstairs, end of the hall past the card parlor," she replied. "We'll have cake and a breakfast ready for you and your guests once the ceremony is complete."

David and Marian exchanged glances of surprise. "That's very kind of you," David said.

"Well, this is the Soho Club. If we couldn't see to marrying the couples who meet under our roof, then we wouldn't be doing our jobs now, would we?"

Marian beamed in delight. "Would you know the whereabouts of Lord Penhurst? I should like him to know about the arrangements."

"You'll find him and the viscount in the card parlor. It's rather quiet in there this morning as most of our other guests have departed."

"Thank you," David said as he offered Marian his arm.

They made their way down the stairs and were about to enter the card parlor when they overheard Richard make a comment. Both stopped short.

Marian's eyes rounded as she stared at David.

David furrowed his brows and scoffed.

"Is it true?" Marian asked in a whisper, her eyes brightening with tears.

Shaking his head, David said. "How could it be?"

CHAPTER 11
WHAT YOU DON'T KNOW

a moment earlier

"Rather fortuitous Engleston played his part so well, wouldn't you say?" Richard, Earl of Penhurst, remarked as he plucked a card from the deck. "I expect I'll be free of my ward by this time tomorrow."

"You could have been free of her if she'd agreed to marry *me*," Marcus, Viscount Huntley, countered, rolling his eyes when the card he selected made his hand even worse than it already was.

"But then you'd be married, and I would have to listen to you complain about her every time we were at the club," Richard said as he spread out his hand on the table. "Show your cards."

The viscount huffed, tossing his hand on the felt table top. "I have nothing, and now I'm bored."

Richard pulled his chronometer from his waistcoat pocket. "They should be back soon," he said. "Unless Engleston has decided to take her to Gretna Green instead of springing for the special license."

"He's too honorable for that," Marcus stated. "He's

probably left her virtue intact. I bet they didn't even spend the night under the same roof."

Giving the viscount a quelling glance, Richard got to his feet and headed for the door. He stopped short when he rounded the corner, though.

His niece and the baron were engaged in a discussion that had Marian in tears and David doing his best to keep her from running off.

About to join them, Richard paused when David noticed his arrival and scowled at him. At the same time, Marian ran for the stairs.

"Damn you," David stated before he hurried to follow her.

A few moments earlier
Marian regarded David with a look of disbelief. "My uncle put you up to this?" she asked in dismay "What? Did he offer you double my dowry to be rid of me?"

"No. Not at all," David replied, attempting to sort what they had overheard in the card parlor. "I had no idea you even existed when I arrived yesterday."

"I should have known this was too good to be true," Marian replied, her lips quivering as tears streamed down her face.

"But it is true. What we have, I mean," David sputtered. "I love you. I want to marry you—"

"For the money, I'm sure," Marian wailed before she ran for the stairs.

Stunned at her sudden departure, David glared at Richard. "I played my part?" he repeated in disbelief.

"Now, now, it's not like that," Richard said in an attempt to calm the baron. "It's just... it worked out so well, you two meeting one another like you did—"

"She asked me if I was her betrothed," David remembered. "Before we were even introduced."

Richard angled his head back and forth. "I might have suggested you were in the market for a wife," he hedged. "And that you two would make a perfect couple, seeing as how you're both so shy," he added with a pained expression.

David huffed. "Damn you," he stated before he hurried off after Marian. He knew where he could find her—she would be in the room at the end of the hall. But how would he convince her he had nothing to do with how they had met? How would he convince her he hadn't been part of some sort of set-up? That he wasn't marrying her for her dowry, even if he might require it until the weather improved?

"The truth is always best."

David whirled around to discover Mrs. Skarsgard standing at her office door. Her arms were crossed over her chest and her head was angled to one side as if she had paid witness to a dozen similar situations in her position as proprietress of the Soho Club.

"And if she's still not convinced I wish to marry her? That I wasn't part of some nefarious scheme concocted by her damned uncle? Excuse the curse, please."

Mrs. Skarsgard took a deep breath and let it out. "A few kisses should help alleviate the issue," she replied. "We'll meet you in the chapel in fifteen minutes."

David blinked. He had almost forgotten about the wedding ceremony.

Determined to set things straight with Marian, he marched to the end of the corridor and stood before the door. He thought about asking to be let in but decided she would only tell him to go away.

He thought to break down the door. Make a show of force to convince her he was sincere in his affections.

About to put a shoulder into the wood panel, he tested the door handle and found it unlocked. Girding his loins, he opened the door and winced. Marian was face first on the bed, her sobs apparent in how her shoulders shook. The bouquet of flowers had been abandoned on the dresser.

David made his way to the bed and sat down on the edge of it.

"How dare you?" she whispered when she realized he was there.

He leaned over and kissed her forehead. "I dare because I love you, and I wish to be your husband," he said.

A sob robbed her of breath for a moment. "How much is he paying you?" she asked as a new round of tears began.

Grimacing, David shook his head. "I have no idea what your dowry is," he replied. "He never said, and I didn't ask." He pulled a handkerchief from his pocket and offered it to her. "It wouldn't matter, though. I want to marry you so much, I wouldn't even require a dowry, except I would like for you and the children to have a decent settlement upon my death."

Marian's gasp was quickly followed by a sob. "Ch... children?" she repeated.

He nodded. "As many as you'd like, of course," he said.

When she didn't respond but only hiccuped, he pulled her into his arms and settled her on his lap. "Yesterday, when you asked if I was your betrothed, I was dumbfounded. It was such an unexpected question from such a beautiful young woman. I was so shocked and so happy, how could I say anything but 'yes'?" he asked.

Marian furrowed her brows. "My uncle didn't speak with you about marrying me?" she asked between hiccups.

David shook his head. "He did not. He didn't mention it in his letter to me, either. I didn't even know you were Dickey's niece until we were in the card room yesterday."

Dipping her head, she scoffed. "So a girl asks if you're her betrothed, and you... you just say 'yes', without... without so much as... as an introduction?" she asked, her query interrupted by sobs.

Screwing up his face in a grimace, David nodded. "I did. I couldn't help myself," he admitted. "But I promise you, it will never happen again."

"Oh?" she asked, her eyes rounding. Disappointment appeared in her expression.

"Well, of course not. The woman who is going to marry me in five minutes is right here on my lap. And she's about to kiss me." He took his handkerchief from her and dabbed her cheeks.

"She is?"

He nodded. "Marry me, Marian. You took my virtue. Now make me an honest man," he whispered.

She leaned in and kissed him on the corner of his mouth, but he was quick to take advantage and kissed her on the lips. When he finally pulled away, he sighed. "I can hardly wait to make love to you again," he whispered. He glanced around the room, remembering her comment about the pink decor. "You won't even notice we're surrounded by pink," he added softly.

"Promise?" she asked as another sob robbed her of breath for a moment.

"I do." David wasn't about to tell her how much he looked forward to seeing her naked again, no matter what color room they were in.

She took a deep breath and used the handkerchief to wipe away the rest of her tears. "I'll make an honest man out of you, David Engleston." She gave him a watery grin.

David sighed in relief as he helped her to stand. Handing her the bouquet of flowers, he offered his arm and the two made their way to the Soho Club chapel.

Although her uncle wasn't present when they entered and moved to stand before the priest, Richard arrived sometime before the vows were exchanged and signed as a witness. He even managed to kiss the bride on the cheek while Mrs. Skarsgard added her signature to the marriage certificate.

"I apologize for the misunderstanding," Richard said as they made their way to the dining room. Huntley was already there, a footman seeing to his breakfast. "But as I recall, I did warn you that you would be meeting your betrothed here," he added, his attention on his niece.

Marian dipped her head, deciding she didn't wish to argue. "You did," she murmured, once again wiping away tears from her cheeks.

Tears of happiness.

"Do be sure to see to it my dowry is paid," she added.

Richard winced. "I will see to it on the morrow," he promised, deciding it would be some time before he would be back in his niece's good graces. He moved to sit with Lord Huntley.

"Would it be possible for a slice of the cake to be sent to my husband's mother?" Marian asked of Mrs. Skarsgard. "She's in Brighton."

"I'll see to it as soon as you've finished eating," Mrs. Skarsgard replied. "And I'll have the rest wrapped up for you to take to Engleston Park."

Marian gave her thanks before she rejoined her husband and uncle, surprised the proprietress knew of their plans. Remembering a Soho Club footman had been at the townhouse the evening before, she realized the butler must have relayed the information.

"So, Dickey, when are you planning to marry?" David asked as he held Marian's chair for her.

The earl gave a start. "How... how did you know?" he asked, looking up from his plate in surprise.

Marian and David exchanged knowing glances. "Just a lucky guess," David said with a shrug.

CHAPTER 12
EPILOGUE

One year later, Engleston Park study, Kent
Oblivious to the chaos happening in the Engleston Park kitchens, David lounged on the sofa in his study, one foot on the floor covered by the sleeping sheepdog and his attention on a sheaf of papers he had received from his solicitor the day before. A quick trip to London had afforded him and Marian the opportunity to pay a call at Penhurst Place to meet her uncle's wife of nearly a year and to introduce their son to his great uncle and to his grandmother.

Although he pretended interest in the babe, Richard had his own new addition to show off—a two-month-old baby girl. While the women exchanged talk of caring for their children and households, Richard and David retired to the earl's study. In an effort to clear the air regarding their uncomfortable parting from the Soho Club the year before, Richard poured brandies for them both and admitted he had already decided to remarry when he had arranged for them to meet at the Soho Club.

He knew there would be trouble in his household if he didn't find a suitable husband for Marian.

"It wouldn't have been fair to my niece to have to give up her station as my hostess, but I knew Constance would insist on running the place," Richard said, referring to his new countess. "I knew you needed a wife, and so I mentioned to Marian that I had found her a suitable husband. Thought the Soho Club would be a perfect location in which to begin a courtship," he went on. "And apparently, it was."

David furrowed his brows. "Oh, it was," he agreed. "And I have to admit that if you had let me in on your plans, I don't know that I would have accepted your invitation," he added.

"I knew you wouldn't have, which is why I didn't tell you." Richard angled his head to one side. "I do hope you're not still sore at me."

"Oh, I'm not," the baron assured him. "I could not have chosen a better woman to be my wife if I had attended a Season of entertainments in London," he added. "But it pains me when I think of her shock when she thought I had conspired with you in order to take her off your hands."

Grimacing at the reminder, Richard said, "She let me know she forgives me. The mention of a larger dowry may have helped in that regard."

"Oh, no doubt," David replied. "Which is part of why we're in London today. We came here directly from my solicitor's office. He had the papers ready for both my last will and testament and for the settlement for Marian and the children."

Impressed at hearing the news, Richard said, "Well, you're certainly set." He dipped his head. "I do appreciate you seeing to her future. To her present," he remarked. "She seems very happy."

David nodded. "I intend to keep her that way, sir."

*H*e and Marian had departed Penhurst Place exactly one hour after their arrival. They had stopped at his townhouse to see his mother and then taken her for an ice at Gunter's Tea Shop.

"I was so happy to have received a slice of your wedding cake whilst I was in Brighton," Eva told them.

"You did?" David asked in surprise. He gave Marian a quick glance.

"I might have seen to it a slice was boxed up and sent before we left the Soho Club," Marian said. "Although I don't know how Mrs. Skarsgard knew *where* to send it."

"It was so good, I didn't mind at all that I missed the nuptials," his mother went on, lifting the baby into her arms.

Before they had departed the tea shop, the dowager baroness proudly showed off her grandson to every matron she knew in the establishment before announcing she would be spending the next Season in Bath.

Apparently she knew Marian would be more than capable of running the Engleston townhouse in her absence.

Their last stop in London had been at the Soho Club. Mrs. Skarsgard was happy to meet the babe and reminded them they could return to the club whenever they wished.

*D*avid was wondering when they might next head to London for a stay at the Soho Club—their wedding breakfast had been exceptional, and the wedding cake rather good—when he looked up to discover his wife standing on the threshold of the study. Her eyes were wide before she let out a sigh of relief.

"What is it, my sweet?" he asked in alarm, lowering the papers to reveal a lump atop his chest. He intended to stand upon seeing her, but his effort to sit up was impeded by an additional weight on his body and the slumbering dog draped over his foot.

"I thought your son had gone missing," Marian said as she crossed her arms and angled her head.

"Oh, he's not missing. He's right here," David said as he indicated the bundle on his chest. Wrapped in a blanket, the future seventh Baron Engleston was snoring softly.

"What's he doing there?" she asked as she made her way to stand over the two men in her life.

"Well, he is keeping me warm," David replied. "He's like a huge lump of coal but without the soot and smoke. He did fart a couple of times, though."

Marian tittered. "He is rather warm to hold," she agreed, her initial concern melting away. "And growing heavier by the day."

"Since he was merely sleeping in his bassinet, I thought he could do it on me just as well," David explained, his appreciative gaze taking in his wife's newest yellow gown.

Upon learning from Mr. Tuttlebaum that his fields were due to yield a bumper crop that year, he'd had a modiste in Kent make it for her. The older woman insisted the color wasn't yellow but rather "jonquil."

In honor of the citrus trees in the greenhouses producing more lemons and oranges than expected, David had ordered another gown in a bright yellow-gold muslin the modiste said was "evening primrose." He really didn't care to know the color names as long as the gowns pleased Marian and reminded him of how she had brought sunshine into his life at a time when he needed it most.

"Were... were you in need of him?" he asked, one of his hands moving to the babe's bottom to pull him farther up onto his chest as he sat up on the sofa. Morgan Richard Engleston took exception and let out a cry of complaint.

Her humor still apparent, Marian lowered herself to sit on the edge of the sofa. She placed a kiss on her husband's forehead. "No, but he's going to be in need of *me* at any moment," she warned.

"Again?" David asked in surprise. "He's not that large," he commented, his eyes darting to her swollen breasts.

In bed earlier that morning, as he had nearly every morning since the birth of his heir, he had watched in fascination as the babe suckled her nipples. For the past two months, he had waited patiently every morning for his turn with Marian, determined to pleasure her senseless before their breakfast was delivered. Although he had learned what he could from the books he had found in his library, he was discovering new ways to make love to his wife all on his own. "He must have a bottomless stomach," he remarked.

Marian glanced down her front. "Actually, it's been several hours," she countered. "And he probably needs his nappy changed." She indicated the sheaf of papers David still held in one hand. "What were you reading?"

David winced when the babe stirred again, his tiny feet digging into his ribs. "The final settlement papers," he replied. "Your generous dowry will afford you and our children a rather comfortable living after I'm gone."

The dowry Richard had paid David the day after the wedding had supplemented his income after The Year of No Summer's horrible crop losses and made it possible for Mr. Tuttlebaum to finally ask for Mrs. Wright's hand in marriage.

The housekeeper was at that very moment dressing for the ceremony, and Margaret, the cook, was continuing with the breakfast preparations. A wedding cake had come out of the oven the day before, its sugar icing coating the dense fruit cake in a smooth, white shell.

It was Marian's turn to wince. "Don't be dying anytime soon, my dearest. You promised me more children. Oh, and we need to be leaving for the church soon."

"I don't plan to die," he replied, leaning down to place a kiss on his son's head. He glanced at the clock on the fireplace mantel. "What time is the wedding?"

"Eleven o'clock. Margaret said she would have the breakfast ready to serve at noon," Marian replied, lifting her son into her arms. "The weather will be glorious, so I'll have the footman set up the trestles in the garden," she added. "Come on, my darling son. Let's get you fed and changed."

David grinned as he watched Marian take her leave of the study. He was about to follow her out of the room when his attention went to the window.

He frowned.

Beyond the glass, rain poured from a ceiling of dark gray clouds. He was reminded of the day he had traveled to the Soho Club.

"Glorious?" he repeated to himself. *What could she be thinking?*

But two hours later, as the wedding guests gathered in the gardens behind Engleston Park for a huge breakfast, the blue sky was clear and the summer sun was warming the air. Wearing the same gown she had been wearing the day she had met David at the Soho Club, Marian smiled as she played hostess for her first wedding breakfast.

Standing at the other end of the trestles while conversing with one of his tenant farmers, David was reminded of the first and only day of his betrothal. Of the words they had spoken in the corridor. If he hadn't overcome his shyness to say "hello" to her when she emerged from her room that day, Marian might not have asked the question that led to their marriage.

He captured his wife's attention and crooked a finger.

Intrigued, Marian ended her conversation with one of the villagers to announce that everyone should be seated and to start eating before she joined him. "Yes, my dearest?"

"By chance, are you my betrothed?" he asked, sounding breathless. He held out a small velvet box.

Marian blinked. And blinked again. "Why, yes. Yes I am," she replied happily, taking the box from him. She opened the hinged lid and gasped at seeing a sapphire ring. *"Another ring?"* she asked in surprise.

"Happy anniversary," he said before he kissed her thoroughly.

He was oblivious to the few wedding guests who paid witness, but Frank Tuttlebaum and his new wife took the opportunity to exchange their own kiss at the other end of the table.

Two weeks went by before it rained again.

ABOUT THE AUTHOR

A self-described nerd and student of history, Linda Rae spent many years as a published technical writer specializing in 3D graphics workstations, software and 3D animation (her movie credits include SHREK and SHREK 2). Getting lost in the rabbit holes of research has resulted in historical romances set in the Regency-era as well as Ancient Greece.

A fan of action-adventure movies, she can frequently be found at the local cinema. Although she no longer has any tropical fish, she follows the San Jose Sharks and makes her home in Cody, Wyoming.

For more information:
www.lindaraesande.com
Sign up for Linda Rae's newsletter:
Regency Romance with a Twist
Follow Linda Rae's blog:
Regency Romance with a Twist